"Great run."

The Texas drawl startled Montana. She recognized the cowboy she'd seen watching her from the stock pen.

"Thanks."

He grinned from beneath his straw Stetson, gray-blue eyes studying her with interest. "I'm Luke Holden, a friend of Clint and Lacy's."

"Montana Brown." His handshake was strong, and he was about as cute as they came.

"Clint said you're here to compete in the upcoming rodeo."

He'd been asking about her. The idea sent an unwanted thrill through Montana. "I plan to."

He grinned. "You'll win if that's the case."

Her stomach did a little electric slide at the way it lit his face up. "So, Luke Holden, what do you do in the rodeo?"

"I'm supplying the stock. Speaking of which, I need to get back to it. Nice to meet you, Montana Brown." He tipped his hat, turned and strode toward the exit.

Many women came to Mule Hollow to find a husband, but Montana had no room for complications.

And Luke Holden was one cowboy who had *complication* written all over him.

Books by Debra Clopton

Love Inspired

*The Trouble with Lacy Brown
*And Baby Makes Five
*No Place Like Home
*Dream a Little Dream
*Meeting Her Match
*Operation: Married by Christmas
*Next Door Daddy
*Her Baby Dreams
*The Cowboy Takes a Bride
*Texas Ranger Dad
* Small-Town Brides
  "A Mule Hollow Match"

*Lone Star Cinderella
*His Cowgirl Bride
**Her Forever Cowboy
**Cowboy for Keeps
Yukon Cowboy
**Yuletide Cowboy
†Her Rodeo Cowboy

*Mule Hollow
**Men of Mule Hollow
†Mule Hollow Homecoming

DEBRA CLOPTON

was a 2004 Golden Heart finalist in the inspirational category, a 2006 Inspirational Readers' Choice Award winner, a 2007 Golden Quill award winner and a finalist for the 2007 American Christian Fiction Writers Book of the Year Award. She praises the Lord each time someone votes for one of her books, and takes it as an affirmation that she is exactly where God wants her to be.

Debra is a hopeless romantic and loves to create stories with lively heroines and the strong heroes who fall in love with them. But most important, she loves showing her characters living their faith, seeking God's will in their lives one day at a time. Her goal is to give her readers an entertaining story that will make them smile, hopefully laugh and always feel God's goodness as they read her books. She has found the perfect home for her stories, writing for the Love Inspired line, and still has to pinch herself just to see if she really is awake and living her dream.

When she isn't writing, she enjoys taking road trips, reading and spending time with her two sons, Chase and Kris. She loves hearing from readers and can be reached through her website, www.debraclopton.com, or by mail at P.O. Box 1125, Madisonville, Texas 77864.

Her Rodeo Cowboy

Debra Clopton

Recycling programs
for this product may
not exist in your area.

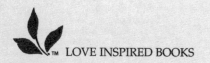 LOVE INSPIRED BOOKS

ISBN-13: 978-0-373-81569-2

HER RODEO COWBOY

www.LoveInspiredBooks.com

Printed in U.S.A.

I know that I have not yet reached that goal, but there is one thing I always do. Forgetting the past and straining toward what is ahead, I keep trying to reach the goal and get the prize for which God called me through Christ to the life above.
—*Philippians* 3:13–14

To Chuck with all my love. God is *so* good.

Chapter One

Her timing was going to stink. Montana Brown wasn't one bit happy about it as she and her horse, Murdock, rounded the last barrel in the arena. They were too far away from the barrel, and it was all her fault. Poor Murdock was giving it his all and she wasn't. Her mind—her focus simply wasn't where it was supposed to be….

It wasn't on the barrels they were running, despite the awesome opportunity she'd been given to train here in this beautiful huge covered arena that belonged to her cousin Lacy Brown Matlock and her husband, Clint Matlock. It was a wonderful place on the outskirts of Mule Hollow—which just happened to be the cutest little Texas town Montana had ever seen. Honestly, she couldn't ask for anything more perfect. But even with all these perfect conditions, instead of concentrating on barrel racing, her mind kept going where she did not want it to go...her dad.

"Focus, Montana," she muttered, feeling her horse's muscles bunch and gather beneath her as the powerful animal cleared the barrel. Digging her heels, knowing they needed all the speed they could gain, she urged Murdock to give it one last shot of speed as they raced toward the timer.

Forgiveness. The word snapped into her thoughts like the pounding of Murdock's hooves. She'd been thinking about this place since she'd gotten up that morning, and her riding showed it. *How do I forgive him—*

"Stop," she commanded through clenched teeth. *"Focus!"* Shoving all thoughts away, she tried to concentrate on moving with Murdock. No doubt about it, yes, sir, her timing was going to be as rank as a skunk on a windy day!

Crossing the time line, she pulled on the reins and leaned back with Murdock as the gray dug his hooves into the dirt and slowed. Cringing, she forced herself to look at the digital reading and her heart sank at the number, despite already knowing it wasn't going to be good.

Some might be satisfied with the time; she wasn't some. If she wanted to win, her time had to be better than good.

And Montana Brown was here to win.

This was her shot, and she didn't plan on wasting it. She just had to get her head back in the game.

These last few weeks, so much of her life had been turned inside out.

When Montana quit her job and walked out of her dad's accounting firm, she hadn't known what she was going to do.

Uncertain and confused, she'd called her cousin, Lacy Matlock. Lacy had insisted Montana come stay with her and her husband Clint. The small town of Mule Hollow where she lived was holding a huge homecoming rodeo in a month, and Lacy wanted Montana competing in it. She'd even insisted Montana could help take care of their new baby boy, Tate, if she was worried about a job.

Montana had needed a job, but she'd been so angry when she'd quit that she hadn't really given it much thought and taking care of a sweet baby would be wonderful while she took a chance on reviving her old dream of becoming a professional barrel racer. Believing this was the answer to prayer,

Montana'd packed her bags, stored her things and headed to Mule Hollow.

She was glad to be here. Glad to have family who cared. She could practice all she wanted, and by the time the rodeo started up in three weeks she knew she could be in the running for the win. She needed that. Montana knew as well as Lacy did, that her parents' breakup had affected her deeply.

"Stop thinking about it," she muttered. Leaning forward, she patted Murdock's neck. "Don't you worry, fella, we're going to practice hard so you won't be embarrassed."

As if relieved, he nodded his head and pranced a few feet. Despite their bad score, Montana chuckled. "You are the vainest horse I know and I love you."

And she did. Poor horse had been put out to pasture the last few years as she'd gotten sidetracked with her career. Sidetracked with pleasing her dad and doing what was expected of her. But that was done now. It wasn't an issue anymore.

Forgiveness was.

"Okay, this is ridiculous. Let's go again, Murdock. And this time I'll give it my all, just like you are giving it yours."

Looking up at the huge, covered arena,

she closed her eyes and imagined the stands full of spectators here to watch a competitive rodeo. There was no way she was going to come out here and embarrass herself *or* Murdock by doing a poor job. No way! Breathing in the quietness of the place, she tried to settle her thoughts and focus. "Please, God, help me do this," she whispered. Closing her eyes once more, she let the silence of the huge space fill her senses.

Opening her eyes, she set her lips in a firm line and her sights on the barrels.

She was going around those barrels again; but this time she was going at them like the cowgirl she used to be.

The cowgirl that she'd come back to Mule Hollow to find.

And to do that, she'd better get her head on straight, concentrate and stop letting this forgiveness issue wage war on her.

Because forgiveness just wasn't in her heart right now.

"The cowgirl can ride." Luke Holden propped a boot on the bottom rung of the arena fence, as he watched the horse and rider practically fly at the speed of light from one barrel to the next. The horse and rider seemed to move as one. The woman, who looked to be in her mid-twenties, was pretty in a girl-next-door sort of way. She had dark hair the color of a bay horse's mane that glistened in the overhead lights of the arena, and it hung in a short braid from beneath her straw cowboy hat. She was focused and intent as she urged her horse on.

"Yes, she can. That's Lacy's cousin, Montana Brown," Clint Matlock said without looking up from the clipboard. He was studying the list of livestock Luke would be providing for the upcoming Mule Hollow Rodeo. "She's staying with us for a while and plans on competing in the barrels at the rodeo. Lacy says she hasn't been riding for a few years, but ever since she got here a week ago, she's spent hours on her horse."

"It shows. She's good."

"Evidently, she was well on her way to the national level when she quit to concentrate on college a few years back. She could still be great."

Watching her as she crossed the time line, Luke saw her frown at the digital reading—which he couldn't see from his vantage, but knew had to be good. "No doubt about that.

I'd never have known she hasn't been riding." He shot a grin at Clint. "The other competitors better be on their game."

"No kidding," Clint agreed, glancing up, then back to the list.

Luke decided it'd be a good thing to get his mind back on business and not the cowgirl. "Do you think that'll do it?"

"It looks great." Clint handed the clipboard back to him. "You have first-rate stock. These rodeos are going to be a big draw to everyone around. Including bringing back some hometown folks. It'll be good for everyone, including helping you build a solid reputation with your rodeo stock."

It was true. Mule Hollow was sponsoring three different rodeos over the summer to promote the town, calling them the homecoming rodeos, and he was supplying the stock for them. "I appreciate you putting in a good word for me, so I could get the contracts on all three events. I owe you."

Clint shot him a frank look. "You don't owe me anything. I'm glad to do it. Even after all the years you worked on the ranch with me, I'm doing this because you deserve it."

"I learned from the best."

Clint nodded, looking thoughtful. "Yeah, my dad knew his stuff."

Luke had learned much from Mac Matlock, but he'd learned a lot from Clint, too. Though Clint was only a few years older than Luke, the guy had been working beside his dad since he was barely old enough to ride. He had a relationship with his dad that Luke envied. "Don't sell yourself short. You know a few things yourself. That's why this ranch is what it is today. Mac taught you well."

The Matlock Ranch was one of the biggest, most successful ranches in the region. It was his legacy, something he would pass on to his son someday. Luke was aiming at building something similar, if all went as planned. These rodeos were going to help his finances and his reputation grow.

"It's going to be a busy summer, with all of the town involved in these homecoming rodeos."

Clint gave him a don't-I-know-it look. "The gals are gonna drive us all crazy."

"No doubt about that. I saw Esther Mae yesterday, and she was buzzing at a hummingbird's pace with her plans." Esther Mae was in her sixties and fairly excitable when it came to…well, pretty much everything.

"Lacy's pretty excited, too. But you know her, she loves to plan all these festivals. And I have never been able to keep up with the woman."

Luke agreed. Mule Hollow had been hosting all manner of festivals, dinner theaters—you name it, they had it. The place had been alive with activity ever since Esther Mae and her two friends came up with a plan to save their beloved town from dying. A few years ago, they'd advertised for ladies to come to town and marry all the lonesome cowboys. Lacy had arrived and supercharged their idea with her own kind of energy—falling in love with Clint in the process. To the men's surprise, the ladies' idea had worked above and beyond what any of them had anticipated, totally astounding all the men in town.

These rodeos were their latest idea. But this was a little different. These three rodeos, one a month stretching out across the summer, were geared to bringing home "the runaways" as Clint called them. The good folks of Mule Hollow wanted family and friends who had moved away to come home and see how much the town had changed. They wanted some familiar faces to move back to town and, like Esther Mae, everyone seemed extra excited about the summer events. Esther Mae, Norma Sue and Adela, known as the matchmaking posse, had zeroed in on anybody they could "help out" where love was concerned. They'd tinkered with him a time or two, but probably decided he was a lost cause. Luke just wasn't ready to look for love, and no one could change his mind about that until he was good and ready.

He wondered if Montana Brown was here looking for love. Looking to find a lonesome cowboy and make the posse's matchmaking dreams come true. If she wasn't, she'd sure better watch out.

"Speaking of all of this, Luke, you've been around from the beginning and you're still single. What's up with that?" Clint asked.

"Determination, that's what." Luke laughed.

"Maybe so," Clint said, grinning. "Hey, I've got to get to Ranger and a bull show at the stock barn. Thanks for coming by with this. We'll talk more, but in the meantime, you set up in here however you think is right. And…" He'd started to head out but paused, grinning again. "I'm wondering how much longer that determination of yours is going to hold out. The way I see it, you and those brothers of yours have been holdouts way too long. Your time is running out, my friend. Love's a beautiful thing, you might want to try it someday."

Luke looked over to watch Montana make another run. He had to admit that just driving into town did tend to lift his spirits. But make him want to jump on the bandwagon and find a wife?

No way.

He had a new ranch to build and grow, and a new livestock business to get up and running. He was driven to make something out of himself, and wasn't slowing down until he did it. He'd scrimped and saved like many of his friends, and on a cowboy's pay, that wasn't easy. A wife and family…maybe later. And maybe not.

Right now, he had a good life. He dated some when he felt like it, but it was never ever serious.

He was focused, happy and determined to be better than his dad expected him to be. And nobody, not even the matchmaking posse, could change that.

Watching Montana round the last barrel again, he saw grit and determination in her expression. He found himself curious about what motivated her. What put that fire in her eyes that flashed as she leaned in low and thundered toward her mark?

"Great run."

The Texas drawl startled Montana as she walked around the corner of the arena's fence, heading toward the stall with Murdock in tow. She recognized the cowboy as one she'd seen watching her from the stock pen. She'd ignored him up till now. He'd been talking with Clint earlier, but hadn't left when Clint did. Too bad. She'd been determined not to let him break her concentration. She'd had a horrible morning run, but then she'd found her focus and made some decent runs.

"Thanks," she said, slowing so she wouldn't be rude. He grinned from beneath his straw Stetson, a flash of white teeth standing out against his darkly tanned skin. He had a lean face, prominent cheekbones and a jawline that seemed chiseled from stone. He looked like a man who knew his own mind. The laugh lines around his eyes told her he knew how to smile, even if he looked like a fairly serious dude.

"You're welcome. You sure can fly on that

horse." He tipped the brim of his hat, as intriguing brown eyes studied her with interest. "I'm Luke. Luke Holden. I'm a friend of Clint and Lacy's."

He held out his hand and Montana shook it briefly. "I'm Montana Brown. It's nice to meet you." His handshake was strong and his hand callused. From the look of him, she figured he did some kind of cowboy work. Not that she was interested. Even if he was about as cute as they came. Even if she had to admit that God hadn't held back when he'd put Luke Holden together. The solid-as-a-redwood cowboy was impressive.

"Clint said you were Lacy's cousin, and you're here to compete in the upcoming rodeo."

He had been asking about her. The idea sent an unwanted thrill through Montana. She frowned at the feeling. "I plan to. I've got a long way to go, though."

He grinned. "You'll win, if that's the case."

Her stomach did a little electric slide at the way his smile lit his face up. "I'll give it my best shot," she said, trying hard to ignore the attraction sparking between them. She patted Murdock's neck. "I can't let Murdock down," she said with a wink, that just sort of slipped out on its own. "He's working way too hard for that. Isn't that right, ole boy?" As if understanding exactly what she was saying, the big gray nodded his head and snorted.

Luke's smile spread slow and easy across his face, lifting his cheekbones higher and causing his eyes to spark with unmistakable teasing interest. *And why not? You winked at the man.*

"He's a competitor, that's for sure," Luke said. "But you've obviously got some fight in you, too."

Why had she winked at the man? Crazy was what she was. Just looking at him made her cheeks flush. But there was no stopping her curiosity about the cowboy.

"So, Luke Holden, what do you do in the rodeo?" There was nothing wrong with asking that, right? The guy was cute and his grin was unhinging—but the buck stopped there.

"I'm supplying the stock. I've never competed myself. I was always too busy working. Speaking of which, I need to get back to it. Nice to meet you, Montana Brown." He tipped his hat and returned her earlier wink with his own. "Ride hard and hang tight. You're gonna blow them out of the water." That said, he turned and strode toward the exit.

Montana watched Luke as he left, his stride strong, no hesitation and no looking back over his shoulder at her…unlike herself who stood there gawking when she should be taking care of business.

"Come on, Murdock, time to rest. Tomorrow we're going twice as hard so we can at least make a decent showing."

Despite her determination not to, she looked over her shoulder once more, but Luke Holden was gone.

Something about him lingered, and Montana found her thoughts continually turning back to him as she brushed Murdock down.

And that just would *not* do. Many women came to Mule Hollow to find a husband. But Montana had come to find herself. To do that, there was no room for complications.

And Luke Holden was one cowboy who had *complication* written all over him.

Chapter Two

"How's my little Tater-poo?" Montana cooed, taking Tate from Lacy. The six-month-old was all cuddly and warm. "He's getting to be a hunk."

"Tell me about it." Lacy handed over the bottle that she'd been feeding him. "He eats like his daddy, don't cha, little man?"

"Hey, he's a growing boy."

"So true! You finish feeding my sugar pie while I get the rest of my grocery list made out. Guess I should tell you that we're having a barbecue this weekend."

"We are?" Montana settled into the rocker as Tate attacked the bottle with gusto. "Why? What's the occasion?"

"For you, silly. I want everyone to come meet you, that's why."

Montana was startled by this information. "Do you have time for that? I mean, I thought you had a lot of planning to do for the rodeo?"

"Oh, we've got that handled," Lacy said, brushing the thought away with the wave of her pink-tipped fingers. "The matchmaking posse's got that under control. Things are rolling right along with the rodeo and the festival we're going to have in conjunction that same weekend. Yep, we've got food vendors coming, and Cort and Lilly Wells always head up a petting zoo with their adorable donkey, Samantha. All kinds of fun stuff is getting ready to happen this summer. It's going to be great," she said with gusto. "But first we're having *your* barbecue."

A lump formed in Montana's throat. She loved her cousin. That was all there was to it. She fought to steady her voice. "You know, you've really helped me when I needed it the most."

Lacy's brilliant blue eyes twinkled as they looked to Montana's and held. "I was concerned for you. You know God loves you more than I do—though I love you like a sister, and wouldn't give you up for anything in the world. But it's true, He does. And I was concerned that you were forgetting that, with all this drama you're going through. I needed to help you know that."

That was Lacy, so strong in her faith. "I'm not going through it anymore. If my mother and my dad want to get divorced, that's their business." If she said it out loud, then maybe it would be true. The anger she felt over everything that had happened welled up inside of her once more. When would it end?

"You know, Montana, people let you down sometimes. That's just the way it is. But God never does," Lacy said, as if reading her thoughts.

Montana knew how strong Lacy's faith was, but right now she didn't want to hear about how wonderful God was. She was angry at everyone—including God. "I really don't want to get into this right now. Is that okay?"

"Sure thing. That's fine. You're here to relax and to love my precious baby boy all you want. And to win that rodeo."

She was ready to talk about something else and grabbed hold. "Poor Murdock is so ramped up. He can feel that we're getting ready for something. Poor horse has missed the barrels. But he's doing so well, it's like he was out in the pasture practicing while I was off at school."

Montana rubbed her face against Tate's neck and he grabbed her hair, making her laugh as she disentangled herself from him. One day she was going to have a baby like Tate, and she wasn't going to make him feel guilty for having dreams different from her own. She was going to love him and help him as he went after those dreams.

"This is 'the good stuff,' Lacy."

"Yes, it is," Lacy chirped. "I'm so happy, I really, really am. I wish you'd find someone like my Clint." She grinned mischievously. "But all in God's timing."

Montana was happy for her cousin. She and Lacy had always been a lot alike. Neither of them really needed a man to make them happy, and yet, there was no denying that Lacy seemed more content now. "Lacy, honestly, I'm so mad at my dad right now, and his lying, that I don't even want to think about letting a man in my life."

"I know, and you have every right to be upset. But I'm praying you'll get over that. All men don't lie. Some men happen to pride themselves on being honest, and that's the kind of man God's going to send your way."

Montana gave Lacy a scowl. "He better not send him anytime soon, or it won't matter. I'm not interested in any man but this little man *right* here." She cuddled Tate, burying her face in his chubby neck.

"You, my dear cuz, have good taste. By the way, I saw Luke Holden was here earlier. Did you meet him?"

The cowboy's image whipped into her mind like a red flag. "Yes," she said warily.

"Well, what did you think of him? I happen to think he's a real cutie pie and a real fine man, too."

Surely she wasn't thinking… "Lacy, I told you I'm not interested. I'm here to win a rodeo, not a man."

Lacy stuffed a fist to her hip, her eyes dancing. "Yep, yep, yep," she sang. "You thought he was cute. I *knew* it!"

Montana gasped. "I didn't say that."

"Didn't have to. Your refusal to answer my question said it all."

"Okay, he isn't hard on the eyes. But don't go getting any ideas." The fact that Lacy might be having ideas about her and Luke had Montana's nerves rattling a bit.

"Oh, I'm not promising anything. I was just checking your pulse." Lacy smiled mischievously.

Montana lifted Tate into the air and looked up at his cherub face. "Tell your momma that my pulse is just fine, and you're the only man I'm gonna be interested in for a good long while." She shot Lacy a teasing but serious glare. "And I mean that. Got it, *cuz?*"

"You seen her?"

Luke was sitting at the counter in Sam's diner, waiting on his breakfast. It was 6:00 a.m. and the crowd hadn't bombarded the tiny diner yet—but they'd be in at any moment. Applegate Thornton and his buddy Stanley Orr were already glued to the chairs at the window table. It was their usual morning spot to spit sunflower seeds at their spittoon, play checkers and get in on the happenings and business of everyone in town. Today they were starting with him.

Applegate spit two sunflower seed shells into the old brass spittoon then repeated his question again loudly, as if Luke was the one who was hard of hearing instead of he and Stanley.

"Did you see her yet? Montana Brown. Lacy's cousin."

Oh, he'd seen her all right. And he'd been thinking about her since. "Yes, sir, I saw her yesterday. She was practicing the barrels out in the arena when I was there going over the stock list. Why?"

App shrugged nonchalantly, looking about as convincing as a little kid trying to sneak a cookie. "I was jest wonderin'. She's a cute little thang. And a real good rider. We saw her the other day, too. She knows her way around a horse."

"That's fer shor." Stanley paused, coughing as he studied the checkerboard. Not as chipper as usual, he scratched his balding head. The two men were in their seventies and about as hard of hearing as a tree stump. Though it was questionable whether they just had selective hearing, because they kept tabs on everyone's business.

"Yup," he continued. "She rode that horse of hers out into that arena like greased lighting. I ain't never seen a gal ride—" He suddenly paused and jumped his red checker over App's. "Gotcha, ya old coot."

App's frown deepened, making his thin face droop into a ripple of expanding wrinkles. "I was wonderin' when you was gonna make that move. I wasn't payin' attention when I made that thar mistake."

"Ha, you're jest gettin' whupped. As usual."

App snorted, "I don't always lose, and you know it." Ignoring his turn to move, he kept his attention on Luke. "I heard Lacy was throwing a barbecue this weekend in honor of her cousin. You goin'?"

Lacy had called him last night and invited him and any of his brothers who might happen to be in town. She'd sounded excited about the party. He had to admit that he was looking forward to it himself. "Yeah, I'm going. It'll be nice to help her get to know all of us."

"You oughtta ask her out," App continued. "You know, make her feel welcomed and all."

"That'd shor be nice of ya." Stanley coughed again, glaring at App. "Times a wastin', I'm gonna be dead before you start playin' this here game."

Taking that as his clue to close the conversation, Luke spun his stool back toward the counter. Sam came out of the back in that moment. His short bowlegs were moving as he hustled through the swinging café doors from the kitchen. He slapped Luke's plate in front of him. "Eat up, Luke. Yor gonna need yor strength."

"Why's that?" he asked, hoping App and Stanley had decided to play checkers instead of delve further into his love life. He'd already been thinking about asking Montana out, but he didn't need anybody's help where that was concerned.

Sam gave him a weathered grin. "'Cause my Adela and the gals are countin' on them animals of yours to be in tip-top shape. They want them bull riders comin' in droves fer all the rodeos." It went unsaid that bull riders and bull riding drew women. That was what "the gals" wanted. The gals being the matchmakers of Mule Hollow, Esther Mae Wilcox, Norma Sue Jenkins and Sam's wife, Adela Ledbetter Green.

There was no need for them to worry. "I've got Thunderclap entered, and his reputation attracts riders. They always do wherever he happens to be."

"That's good. Norma Sue and Esther Mae are about ta drive me pure crazy with their planning and carrying on. Adela's even having trouble keepin' them corralled. Why, they're strategizin' about every kin folk they can think of who might be comin' fer the rodeos. I'm telling y'all, that little gal Montana Brown's got a number on her back—and it ain't her barrel racin' number, either. So, jest a word of warnin', in case you ain't figured that out already. If you ask that one out, you might have a big ole bull's-eye show up on yor back, too."

The back of Luke's neck began to itch. "They've tried that a time or two with me, and realized I'm not interested in anything long-term.... You know I'm honest with everyone I go out with about that."

Not saying anything, Sam poured him another cup of coffee and started to go tend to his other customers. Mornings were busy, and he usually worked them alone, till his help came in around eight. But as busy as he was, he held his position, his eyes narrowing as he looked at Luke.

"It's true. Ever'body knows you're a straight shooter on that topic. But—" he grimaced "—from what I hear, that ain't makin' at least one person too all-fired happy."

Luke had a bad feeling he knew where Sam was heading. "What do you mean?"

Sam leaned in close. "I heard tell that thar artist you went out with a time or two ain't happy at all."

Erica. He'd been honest with her from the beginning, and had only gone out with her twice. On their second date, she'd started talking about looking for Mr. Right. He shook his head. "Sam, I broke it off with her the instant I realized she was looking for Mr. Right. I don't do forever. I'd told her I wasn't looking to be anybody's Mr. Right. She got all upset anyway, and I didn't know what to do." The woman had actually thrown dishes at him for "dropping her," as she put it. He'd tried to keep his mouth shut, but that hadn't stopped her from giving him the stink eye whenever she saw him. To keep peace, he'd been trying to steer clear of her, and hoped that soon her anger would blow over. One thing was certain, they weren't compatible, and he was more than glad of it. He didn't like all the drama that came with a woman like that. He'd just missed the signs.

"If you were honest, then you ain't got nothin' ta hold yor head down about. Some women are jest plain high-strung. Now, women like my Adela, well, that's a prize. You jest keep bein' honest. It'd be a shame fer you ta miss out on love. The posse might jest have ta fix that fer you."

"Sorry, Sam. Like I said, I know my own

mind and if I decide to ask Montana out, everything will be just fine. Don't you worry about me. Or her. She'll know right off the bat that I'm not looking for anything serious."

Sam's eyes crinkled at the edges. "One of these days, one of them dates is going ta wrap her finger around yor heart, and then you won't be so cocky about how good you are at walkin' away."

Luke took a bite of biscuits and gravy. He wasn't being cocky. He was being honest. He had plans. Goals. Nothing was getting in his way.

Sam hiked a busy brow. "Yup, that cockiness is gonna be yor downfall. Mark my words, son. Yor time's a comin'."

Chapter Three

"Well, well, hello, Luke Holden. How's life treatin' ya?"

Luke grinned at Montana's perky, playful greeting. They were standing near a fragrant rose bush at Lacy's. The shadows from the oil lantern cast a soft glow on Montana's skin—she looked beautiful. "I'm fine, Montana. Life's fine. I can't complain. How about you? Enjoying the party?" He'd arrived at the barbecue at the Matlocks' a little while earlier, and mingled while Montana made the rounds talking with groups of people Lacy had introduced her to. He'd caught her looking at him a few times across the crowd. Something about her drew him, and he got the feeling she was just as curious about him.

She took a sip of sweet tea, watching him

with steady blue-green eyes. "The party—it's good."

"I agree." He caught that she didn't say anything about how life was treating her and he wondered about that. "How's your riding going?"

"Okay. Murdock's a little happier with me today. He wants to win, and he knows the problem is me."

"You always this hard on yourself?"

"Always."

Thoughtful eyes held his. He smiled at her. "Seriously, you need to relax." Man, did she ever. "I saw you laughing a few minutes ago, so I know you can do it."

She laughed then. "Hey, I do laugh now and then, but I'm dead serious when I say I'm always hard on myself. I expect a lot of me." She paused and her eyes drilled into him. "I bet you expect a lot of yourself, too."

"And what gives you that idea?" He liked the way she seemed sure of herself. Sure of her impression of him. He wondered if she was that sure of everything in her life.

"Well, you just do. From what I understand, you have a ranch and cattle and livestock. Plus, you have Thunderclap, your prized rodeo bull. You, Mr. Holden, are a busy man who reeks of expectations."

Had she been asking about him? "I like to keep busy and yes, you're right, I expect a lot of myself. If I don't, then who will?"

"Right. Then again, if your dad was anything like mine, he expected plenty from you."

He gave a derisive grunt. "I can tell you our dads were nothing alike. Mine expected little of me."

Her eyes widened. "What do you mean?"

Luke didn't talk about his dad much, and he wasn't sure why he'd done so now. He'd given her a glimpse into his past that he didn't like thinking about, much less discussing. "Little, as in nothing. My dad didn't push me to be anything but a failure."

"I'm so sorry," she said sympathetically.

"Hey, low expectations drive some harder than high expectations." He gave her a teasing smile to throw off the seriousness of his words. "So, what about you? Your dad expect you to be the best barrel racer in the country?"

"Hardly. He expected me to be valuable to the human race, and that had nothing to do with racing around barrels on a horse."

He grimaced. "Rough. From watching you ride, all I can say is you must have been one rebellious child."

That made her choke on her tea. He moved toward her and patted her on the back. "Didn't mean to choke you up."

"I'm fine," she said after a second. "But let's just say neither one of us is doing very well on reading each other's background."

"So you weren't rebellious? I'm shocked."

That made her eyes twinkle. "I wish. Hard-headed, but not rebellious." She frowned, crinkling her eyebrows in a cute way. "I can't say there haven't been many days that I have deeply regretted my lack of rebelliousness."

He wasn't sure if she was teasing or serious.

She winked at him. "But I'm making up for it now."

That had him even more curious than ever about what was going on behind her pretty eyes. Before he could dig a little deeper, Esther Mae came walking over. The redhead wore a bright green shirt and matching pants that ended just above her ankles.

"Yoo-hoo! I'm so glad y'all are getting to visit. I told Norma Sue and Adela y'all looked so cute standing over here together that I hated to disturb y'all, but one of the kids said the horses in the stall barn were making all kinds of noise. I thought you might want to go check on your horse, Montana."

Montana was instantly alert. "I appreciate the heads-up." She dropped her paper cup in a trash can and was walking down the steps before Luke had time to react.

"Well, don't just stand there, Luke. Go help her."

Luke's eyes narrowed, and he caught the flash of mischief in Esther Mae's spunky green eyes. Instantly, he shot her friends a glance where they were all huddled up on the lawn. Oh, brother, they were all watching, Lacy included. She grinned and waved, then laughed in delight. So much for subtlety.

He gave Esther Mae a look that said he knew exactly what she was up to, then hurried after Montana. She was already halfway across the yard that separated the main house from the arena and horse stalls. Clint didn't keep all of his horses in the arena; instead, he kept them in the barn that was on the back side.

The cowgirl obviously didn't have a clue that she'd just been hoodwinked. Her boots scraped on the gravel as she quickstepped toward the barn. He wondered what her reaction would be to know she'd just been set up. He'd already decided, before the matchmaking effort, that he was going to see if she'd like to go to dinner. Now would be a good time to ask.

The barn was quiet. No sounds of restless horses or anything else for that matter. The arena was a huge covered building with stadium seating on both sides, and a concession stand area and an announcer's box at the front. There were stock pens both front and back, and an area on the outside connecting them. Murdock was stabled at the front, behind the stock pens and announcer's box. The huge building was quiet and lonesome in the late evening. Ahead of him, Montana reached Murdock, put her hand to her hip, looking left then right. Murdock gave her a contented snort as she slowly turned on her heel and stared at Luke. Her eyes flashed like glass in the muted overhead lighting. Her eyes narrowed.

"First of all, this area is way too off the beaten path for the kids to have heard any ruckus—unless they'd been back here causing it. Second, I don't see any signs that Murdock's been the least bit distressed recently."

He couldn't help the grin that tugged at his mouth. "I'd—"

"*I'd* say," she broke in before he could begin, "that there's something fishy in the air."

"And I'd say you catch on slow," he drawled, teasing, "but at least you catch on."

"Oh, so you've had it figured out all along, have you?"

"Pretty much. Of course, you were already halfway across the lawn before Esther Mae stopped talking. I got the benefit of spotting Lacy, Adela and Norma Sue along with the little crowd gathered around them, watching us like we were the drive-in movie of the week."

"That is so not good. I'm going to get my cousin! I love her, but I'm gonna get her good."

He got the feeling she wouldn't like it, but the woman was cute, all hot as a firecracker. Looking near to blowing up, she turned in her frustration and began petting the star between Murdock's eyes—as if the action would calm her nerves.

"Actually, I'd planned on seeing if you'd like to go to dinner Saturday night." The moment the words were out of his mouth, it hit him that it might not be the best time to ask her out.

Montana's hand stilled and her gaze shot to his. "No, thanks. It's nothing personal, but I'm not dating right now."

She was turning him down. So his timing hadn't been good, but he knew when a woman was interested. He'd felt the chemistry between them. "It's not *dating*. It's just *one date*—dinner."

Montana studied him with unsympathetic eyes. "I'll tell it to you straight. You and I both know that one date will stir up those ladies out there. I'm not up for that. I'm here to get my head on straight, win a rodeo and help with the baby. Nothing more. I don't need a bunch of sweet, matchmaking ladies fixing me up with a cowboy...who just happens to be you. Sorry. But no."

He felt slightly insulted. "They know I'm not looking for anything long-term. I've made that clear to them. And every woman I go out with," he clarified, thinking she'd like that better.

Her eyebrows rose slightly. "Lots of them, huh?"

That eyebrow didn't bode well. "What?" he asked warily. "Oh, lots of dates?"

"Lots of women."

"Um, a few."

She crossed her arms and tilted her head slightly, silently assessing him. He felt like a science project.

"I'm sure that knowledge helps you get lots of dates."

He was confused with where she was going with this conversation. "It doesn't hurt. I mean, for someone like you I'm not a risk. I'm just a date. Conversation, company. You know, no strings attached." That didn't sound good, even to him. What was wrong with him? He scrubbed his jaw, thinking suddenly that crawling under a hay bale might be in order, judging from the appalled expression on her face.

"And it works out well for you? All these different women who don't want any strings attached."

Was she teasing him—or was she really irritated by the whole idea? He wasn't sure anymore. "Yeah, it works out great."

She grinned sarcastically. "Good for you," she gushed. "I'll stick to *not* jumping into that." She gave him a pat on the arm, rolled her eyes and headed toward the exit.

He stood there, not sure about what had just happened. "Hey, whoa. Wait up."

She rounded the corner out of sight, her voice rang out singsong, "I don't think so."

The sound echoed in the hall, drawing him. He chuckled and jogged to catch up to her. She was already out in the open and heading up the hill toward the house. Laughter could be heard drifting on the barbecue-scented night air. As if in a hurry to get away from him, she strode with purpose, her boots crunching the gravel as she went, her braid swinging in time to the fast pace.

"What's your hurry?" he asked, skidding on the gravel, coming up beside her.

She slid him a glance. "I don't want to give anyone the idea that you and I lingered in the barn for romantic reasons. That wouldn't be good."

He grinned. The woman tickled him. She was so blunt about things. "No, I guess that wouldn't be good. Might get rumors started, and boy, we wouldn't want that, now, would we?"

"No way." She didn't smile, but he thought she was teasing. "I certainly wouldn't want anyone thinking I was joining your string of random dates."

What did women expect from a guy these days? Just because he wasn't interested in marriage didn't mean he wasn't interested in women. "There's nothing wrong with not settling down. Not being ready for forever." He shifted from one boot to the other.

She hiked a brow. "It's random and cheap."

Her attitude irritated him suddenly. He wasn't doing anything wrong. Hadn't done anything wrong, he reiterated to himself strongly, as she started walking off again.

He followed her, not real happy about the situation but not certain what he wanted to do about it.

The party was in full swing when they reached the backyard. Montana clomped up the deck steps. Distracted by his irritation, he was intent on following her just as he caught movement out of the corner of his eye.

"Luke," Erica said, nothing nice dripping from her words.

"Erica. Um, hi." She didn't look happy. Nope, matter of fact, she looked really unhappy—throw things unhappy. He hadn't expected to see her. But he should have known Lacy wouldn't have left her out of the party.

Montana turned back toward him and met his gaze before connecting with Erica's.

"What are you looking at?" Erica snapped at Montana, right before throwing her soda at him!

Yup, throw things unhappy was about right. One minute he was standing there irritated and confused by Montana's attitude. Now, he was drenched with the contents from Erica's tall glass of Texas *sweet* tea!

"What?" he gasped, blinking through the tea dripping from his eyelashes.

"You two-timing jerk!" Erica huffed, then strode past him, shooting a glare over her shoulder—as if he hadn't already gotten the message.

"Two-timing..." he stuttered. He was well aware that everyone within earshot had heard and witnessed the scene. "We just went on two dates. *Just dates,*" he said, looking at Montana.

A twitch of her lips told him she was fighting off laughter. "Yeah," she managed. "Looks like all that dating is working out well for you, huh?" She winked at him, then strode into the house, leaving him dripping on the deck.

"Everybody's a comedian," he muttered.

It was time to have a serious—and he meant serious—talk with Erica. He was not the marrying type. Never was and most likely never would be.

Chapter Four

Norma Sue Jenkins efficiently blocked Luke's way when he headed toward Erica. A robust ranch woman, Norma Sue was hard to avoid when she wanted your attention. She handed him a dishtowel. "I tried telling Erica you and her wouldn't match up." She looked worried. "This isn't good, Luke."

He glanced past Norma Sue and saw Erica tear out in her small compact car. Wiping the sticky tea from his face he shook his head. "No, Norma Sue, it isn't. I wasn't trying to hurt anyone. I told her straight up that I was just dating. I wasn't looking for forever, and she seemed okay with that. Until the second date, and then she started in on all that Mr. Right stuff."

She patted him on the back. "I know. I know. I told her you weren't looking for love, just companionship. I knew she had her sights set on forever, and I told her you weren't the one to count on for that—"

"I think I'm supposed to say thanks to that."

"It doesn't sound good to me, either, but we both know, up till now, that's where you stand. Erica thought she could change your mind and lied to you about her intentions." Norma Sue frowned, her pink cheeks drooping. "All I've got to say is, you may be in for it. I don't know if you noticed, but Erica is a bit high-strung. She doesn't take rejection too kindly."

The woman had just tossed tea on him. He was standing there drenched. "Yeah, Norma Sue, I get the picture loud and clear."

"I figured you did. Why don't you give her some time to cool off, then I suggest you go see her and try real hard to smooth this out. We aren't used to this kind of trouble going on in Mule Hollow."

"Tell me about it. I'm not used to this kind of trouble, either."

He spent the next hour getting ribbed and teased about the incident. Cowboys loved teasing and giving each other a hard time, so, thanks to Erica, he was probably going to be the brunt of jokes for the rest of the year. The talk at the diner alone was going to drive him crazy. And if Erica thought her actions were going to help her find "Mr. Right" anytime soon in Mule Hollow, she was about to be up a creek without a paddle. Getting a date might have just gotten a whole lot harder for her.

Then he thought about Montana—getting a date might have just gotten harder for him, too. The idea didn't sit well. As he drove home, he figured he had some digging out to do. He didn't like having Erica so angry at him, so he was going to have to smooth that out somehow. Didn't change his feelings though. Norma Sue had been right on the money about them not being compatible— there were just some things that couldn't be changed. He didn't figure you could fall in love with someone you weren't attracted to, but he'd seen plenty of times when people who were in love fell out of love. Or one of the two killed the love that had been shared. Luke had seen that plenty. He'd seen it up close and personal where his parents were concerned—yeah, love could be killed. But there was no way it could be forced. Erica was barking up the wrong tree if she figured he was the one for her. He'd get that straight and he'd get it soon. Surely she would understand where he was coming from.

He wasn't going to feel bad about the situation. He had done nothing but be honest in all of this. Montana might hold it all against him, especially after witnessing the sweet tea scene, but in all honesty, he couldn't figure out why.

Then again, maybe he was missing something....

It was a beautiful day, the morning after the infamous barbecue.

"Come on in," Esther Mae called out as Montana walked into Lacy's Heavenly Inspirations hair salon carrying Tate. Instantly, she was bombarded by the spunky redhead. "Oh, there's our baby boy!" Esther Mae cooed, reaching to take Tate.

"We're glad you came," Norma Sue said, moving to give Tate a hug.

Lacy had Adela in the chair and was snipping away at the dainty lady's short, white hair. "He looks so happy!" Lacy said, smiling in his direction. "You are so good with him, Montana. Thank you so much. He's always in such a good mood with you."

"Ha! It's not me. The little fella likes everyone. Although, we did have a great morning. He loves the playpen we fixed up next to the office." The building that housed Lacy and Clint's arena was one of the nicest she'd been in. She was blessed to have it for her own use. "He played happily all morning while I practiced." Montana could still get her barrel racing practice in while watching Tate in the playpen.

"He's content around you." Adela smiled, her electric-blue eyes warm. "Babies know good people when they're around them."

Esther Mae looked up from where she had sat with Tate in the dryer chair. "Little darling bellows every time Hank comes around. It hurts Hank's feelings something fierce."

"Roy Don was the same way." Norma Sue chuckled. "He started to get a complex about it, until one day Tate took to him—" she snapped her fingers "—like the snap of a finger."

"Men, they get their feelings hurt too doggone easy," Esther Mae said while rubbing noses with Tate. "You aren't gonna do that, are you, my sweet potato pie man?"

Norma Sue grunted. "That Luke should have gotten his feelings hurt last night." She looked at Montana. "He needs a woman in his life, and he has no clue how many women want to be 'that' woman. Why, most every woman who goes out with him is secretly hoping he'll notice them, despite knowing he's not planning to get married. They all find out he's more interested in work and building up that ranch than in building a relationship, and they move on. Who knows, maybe Erica's little hissy fit might have been just what he needed to make him think about taking a woman seriously. About taking his life seriously."

"That's right," Esther Mae interrupted. "Life's too short to only think about building things here on earth. He needs a family to leave that ranch to."

Montana started getting uncomfortable with the conversation.

"It's going to take the right woman to help him see that God has more out there for him than work," she chimed in.

"And how about you?" Norma Sue suddenly turned her attention to Montana. "Don't you think he's one handsome cowboy?"

"I've already had this conversation with Lacy." She met her cousin's mischievous eyes in the mirror. "Yes, he's handsome. But I'm not interested."

"What about living in Mule Hollow?" Norma Sue probed. "Are you interested in maybe making this your home?"

"It's a great place," Lacy said, pausing her cutting the wispy hair around Adela's face. "I'm trying to convince her of that, too. Y'all help me."

Adela smiled understandingly. "That would be lovely, dear. If you moved here, you would have all the time you need to sort out whatever it is that's bothering you."

"And then you could appreciate Luke for the man that he is." Norma Sue looked as if she'd just come up with the best idea of the century.

"Aren't y'all supposed to be having a meeting about the fair on the opening day of the rodeo?" Montana reminded them of the reason she'd come to town. She wanted the conversation to move away from her. And Luke.

Lacy took the cape off of Adela, shaking the loose hair from it. "You're a free woman, Adela," she said, smiling. "We're heading over to the diner now. I just needed to finish Adela's cut first."

"By the way, how's Sheri doing?" Esther Mae called from the dryer chair. "Is she and Pace having fun in Australia, training horses?"

"Yes, they are." Sheri was the nail tech and Lacy's partner in the salon. She'd come to Mule Hollow with Lacy when she'd loaded up her 1958 pink Caddy and drove from Dallas to open her new business. "She said that she was thinking of moving there full-time."

"What?" All the matchmakers gasped.

"Whoa!" Lacy waved her hands to hold off any more outbursts. "I was only teasing. She said she's enjoying Australia but will be back home in Mule Hollow in time for the rodeos. Pace is going to ride broncs."

"Whew, that's a relief," Esther Mae said. "Plus, I need a manicure something terrible."

Adela agreed. "It certainly is. We'd miss her and her frank honesty and dry sense of humor."

"Boy, are you right about that." Norma Sue wagged her kinky gray head. "Talk about a hard one to match up. We didn't think the right cowboy was ever going to come along for that little gal."

"But God always sends the right cowboy

for the right woman. In the right time." Adela hugged Lacy. "Thanks for making my hair look so wonderful! We are so glad God also sends hairdressers to the right towns, too."

Lacy looked pleased. "Oh, He did that." She held her hands out for little Tate. He immediately lifted his arms for his momma. Taking him into her arms, Lacy snuggled his neck with her nose and held him close. "God knew this hairdresser needed to be right here in Mule Hollow, so I could meet Clint. So this sweet baby boy could be born."

Montana's heart tugged with emotion watching them.

"Okay, let's go, gals," Norma Sue said, moving to the door and holding it open. "Let's get over to Sam's. I'm sure we have a big group waiting for us over there."

Montana followed the chattering, excited group, but she couldn't stop thinking about them matching her up with Luke. Montana knew they all meant well. After all, it was easy to see that all their hard work was producing lots of happy couples. And families to fill up the town.

Still, she wasn't buying in.

That's right. It was going to take more than the goodwill of the matchmaking posse to make her see things differently. She knew she would feel that way for a long time.

If they thought Sheri Gentry had been a tough cookie to match up, they were in for a surprise because they hadn't seen nothin' yet.

Luke almost turned around and went back to his truck when he walked into Sam's and saw the crowd. The place was packed! Spotting Montana—and no Erica—he decided to stay. He'd dropped by Erica's apartment that morning to see if he could talk to her, but she hadn't been home. He still couldn't get over the fact that she was so angry with him.

He hadn't made it to the counter to grab a seat on a cowhide stool before Esther Mae called out his name.

"Don't sit over there," she called. "We're discussing the rodeo and festival. We need your input."

Sam grinned from behind the counter. "You came in at the wrong time. Even App and Stanley hightailed it outta here the minute they all came marching in."

Luke looked around the room and realized it was all ladies sitting in the booths on one side of the diner, and the other side was empty. "Looks like I missed the memo."

"Yup. You did that. But yor here now, so you might as well dig in and bear it. I'll brang you a nice, *tall* glass of sweet tea. You want a burger ta go with that?"

"Funny, Sam. Real funny. A burger's fine." He crossed to the table next to the one Montana was sitting at. She didn't look too thrilled to see him.

"Hey, Montana, how are you?" he asked. She might not have a high opinion of him, but that wasn't stopping him. After all, he wasn't a bad guy, and maybe if she'd go out with him she'd see that. At least, maybe she'd see that he hadn't deserved a glass of tea in the face.

"Hi, how's it going," she said, looking uncomfortable.

"Good." He tipped his hat. "Hello, ladies." He pulled a chair from a table, and was very aware of all their eyes on him. As they acknowledged him with hellos, he spoke to most of them individually. Many of them were around his age, and moved here in the last two years and married his friends.

Montana took all the interaction in, and he wondered what she was thinking. These ladies knew he wasn't a horrible person. Maybe this was a good thing.

"How's your morning going?" he asked her, leaning across the space toward her. "Did you get your riding done this morning?"

"I did. Tate watched me from the play area while I took a few runs. He likes watching me and Murdock round the barrels."

Lacy held the little fella, who was standing up in his mother's lap, looking pleased with himself.

He started to ask how old Tate was, when Norma Sue began talking about all the things that were going on the opening day of the rodeo. He settled in, gave a sideways glance at Montana, who was particularly intent on everything Lacy and Norma Sue were saying. Luke hadn't known they were having so many vendors coming in. The dunking booth, pie throwing, cow chip toss, three legged race; the list went on and on. He also didn't know a small carnival was coming to town and setting up in one of the pastures.

"A carnival is coming?" Montana asked, perking up in her seat.

"Yes! Isn't it exciting?" Lacy said. "I wanted to tell everyone today as a surprise. I just found out this morning. It's not a big outfit. Just a few rides."

"I hope there's a Ferris wheel," Esther Mae said. "I just love those things."

"Yes, that's one of the rides, and then there's one of those octopus rides."

Esther Mae gasped. "I love that, too. This is going to be sooo much fun."

Montana nodded and he caught her lips twitch. He decided then and there that he was riding the rides with her. That might be a bigger challenge than getting her to go out to dinner with him.

Meanwhile, Montana kept ignoring him, no matter that he sat just two feet away from her.

Frustrated more than he liked to admit, he got up, made his goodbyes to all the ladies and headed down to pick up some supplies at Pete's Feed and Seed. He was walking back to his truck a little while later when Montana drove past him in one of the Matlock Ranch trucks. She didn't even glance his way.

He almost followed her. After all, he needed to stop by Clint's, and it might as well be now. He finally talked sense into himself and turned his truck toward his place instead. What was wrong with him?

Montana didn't think very highly of him. Following her around certainly wouldn't help matters. Her opinion of him wasn't looking any brighter than Erica's. But truth be told, Montana's opinion had him lying awake long after he'd fed his horses and Rover, his lab.

Yup, Montana Brown had him stumped, and he wasn't at all sure what he was going to do about it.

Chapter Five

On Sunday, Montana let her hair hang loose, put on a red dress and went to church with Lacy. It was quite an experience as she entered the quaint, white wooden church with the tall steeple.

Chance Turner was the pastor of the Mule Hollow Church of Faith, and she'd met him briefly at the barbecue. He was around thirty, handsome and a total cowboy. Instead of a suit, he wore starched jeans, Western belt, starched shirt and cowboy boots. When he greeted her outside, he had on a cream-colored Stetson that he wore low over his eyes. It looked completely at home on his head, as did the rest of the Western attire he wore. She wondered what he would say if she told him about the anger that was rolling around in her gut. The anger toward her father that she couldn't seem to shake. He seemed like he would offer some good advice. As she was leaving the service, the need to talk to someone tugged at her.

She hesitated as she shook hands with him. "It was a great sermon," was all she could bring herself to say.

"Yes, it was," Lacy agreed. "Chance always has a way of looking into hearts and touching on things we need to hear. I'm going to run and get Tate from the nursery. I'll be right back."

She saw a flicker in the pastor's eyes when he looked back at her, as if he knew something was going on in her head—or her heart. Did he realize that she was fighting a war inside?

"I'm glad you enjoyed the service," he said, his smile fading to a more serious one. "Is there anything I can do for you, Montana?"

Her stomach went bottomless. "N…no. I'm fine." *Liar, liar pants on fire*—the childhood chant rang in her ears.

His eyes narrowed slightly, digging, as if he'd heard through her denial. He smiled encouragingly. "I'm sure you are. But if you change your mind, I'm easy to find and I'm always ready to listen."

"Thank you, Pastor Turner."

"We're pretty laid-back here. Call me Chance. Did you get to meet my wife, Lynn?"

"I did, and your boys, too."

He smiled. "You have to watch out for those two."

"They're boys. It was nice to meet you." She turned to leave.

"Remember, if you need to talk, the door is always open. Lynn helps out up here, too, and she's here if you wanted to talk to her."

"I'll remember that. Bye." She couldn't get away quick enough. Her heart was reeling with the heaviness and confusion she was carrying inside of it. What to do?

She was almost running to find Lacy as she rounded the corner, getting away from Chance's knowing gaze. She very nearly ran over Luke in the process.

"Whoa! You running barrels without your horse?" he asked, dodging her, jumping off the sidewalk.

"Um, yes. I mean no." There was nowhere for her to go, though she would have liked to avoid the cowboy. Small towns made avoiding a person hard. But it really didn't matter, she told herself. After all, she'd made her position on dating clear. She hadn't seen him during the service, though she'd been looking around for him—there was no denying that she'd been looking for his handsome face in the crowd.

"You look like you're in a hurry. Is everything all right?"

"Yes. I was going to look for Lacy and then head out. I'm planning on riding this afternoon." Why was she explaining herself? What was it about the man that made her so defensive. Then again, maybe it was the entire morning that made her defensive. Attending church when she'd rather have stayed home and ridden Murdock around endless barrels.

"You have a good day, then," he said, and headed for the parking lot.

She watched him go, startled that he hadn't tried to talk longer.

Startled more because she wished he had....

Luke went straight home after church. His younger brother, Jess, was arriving with a new load of cattle from Fort Worth. It was a good excuse to keep him from thinking about how pretty Montana had looked that morning. She'd had on a red dress that looked great on her—but he thought she'd look fantastic in anything. What was it about the woman that had his head spinning?

Jess pulled into the lot about the time it took Luke to change clothes and get to the stock pens. He watched his brother back the big bull wagon cattle trailer up to the chute— bumping the chute in one try. Luke smiled every time he watched Jess do it, remembering the first time his little brother had made it without having to pull forward and back the big trailer up to the chute a second or third time.

Taller and leaner than Luke, Jess stood at about six-four. Luke and Colt had always called him "the little big brother," because he surpassed them in height before they'd reached high school. Colt was smaller, more compact at five-ten, and built like the bull rider he was. All three brothers were close because they'd banded together in defense of their drunken father's treatment. Watching Jess climb down from the truck, Luke felt a sense of brotherly pride. He was proud to call both Colt and Jess brother.

"Hey, honey, I'm home," Jess teased, walking up and clapping him on the back. It was a joke they all passed between themselves since all three had issues with settling down.

Luke chuckled. "I missed you, too."

"Yeah, that's a lie. From what I hear through the grapevine you've been fairly busy juggling women to have missed your ole brother."

"I should have known you would hear about the tea. You probably almost had a wreck laughing about that one."

Jess gave him a sly sideways glance and nodded. "That I did."

They walked to the back of the hauler. No telling who Jess had heard the story from, but he was sure he'd learn the answer eventually, so he didn't bother to ask.

"You should have known that woman wouldn't take kindly to being dumped."

"I didn't dump anyone. I took her to dinner twice. That's it."

"I saw *marriage-hunter* written all over her the moment I saw her. Why do you think *I* didn't ask her out?"

Luke shook his head and grunted. "She seemed nice, and she told me she wasn't looking for anything but a date."

Jess hiked a brow. "And I'm ready to settle down yesterday."

"I know that's a lie."

Jess chuckled as he slid back the trailer latch and they pulled the gate open.

"Erica's just aggravated her plans didn't work out. She tossed that tea on you because she thought she'd have you wrapped around her finger by the second date, and y'all would be on your way to the altar by the third date."

Surely she hadn't thought that.

"You gotta watch out for some of these gals. They can be conniving when it comes to getting what they want. At first they can put on a show, but down the line they start showing you who they really are. I'm just sayin' you need to watch a little closer, bro, or you might wake up married to—"

"Okay, okay, I get the picture, Jess."

Jess propped a boot on the corral and gave him a skeptical glance.

There was one thing the Holden brothers understood loud and clear—marriage didn't always mean happy or better. Luke was beginning to worry if Jess had backed off completely from the idea of marriage.

"They look good," Luke said, changing the subject back to the yearling heifers moving from the trailer.

"They should, for the price we paid." Jess grinned. "But they're worth it."

"How was Okeechobee?"

"Still deep in the heart of Florida, and one long drive home."

Luke laughed. "You're the one who likes to drive."

"Uh-huh. That I do. Gives a man breathing room. So tell me about this Montana Brown I've heard about."

"Are you sure you've been gone? Not hiding out in the back of my truck?"

Jess cocked a brow and gave a dog-faced grin. "Hey, man, I've got my sources. Sooo? You like her?"

"She's interesting," Luke said.

"I hear you've drawn the attention of the posse." Jess stopped smiling. "You might be in trouble if you aren't careful."

Luke closed the trailer and slapped the lock lever down with a clank. "I'm not worried about those three."

"Maybe you should be. Maybe you need to back off before they latch on tighter."

"They have this rodeo and festival to occupy their time. They won't be concentrating on me for about two weeks. There'll be so much going on then that they'll forget all about me."

Jess laughed as he strode to the freight

liner and climbed up into the seat. "Yeah, you go on and keep that lazy attitude. I figure you'll be married by fall."

"Hardly." Luke scowled as he headed toward his own truck. Montana intrigued him, it was true. But being pushed into marriage by the loveable matchmakers wasn't happening, and his brother good-and-well knew it.

Chapter Six

Luke dropped off some extra panels they'd need to hold the excess stock. Montana was in the barn racing like lightning when Luke went by the arena. Her braid slapped against her back as she and Murdock raced by. She wore a blue-green T-shirt that matched her eyes. Eyes that were completely focused on the barrels. It was not something that had to be done immediately, but it was a good excuse to stop.

She'd gotten her time up even better than it was and she looked more at ease in the saddle than she had the last time he'd watched her. She was concentrating so hard as she came around the last barrel, he figured she probably didn't see him sitting on the top rung of the arena fence. Which was a good thing. She had her mind on her barrels today. On the other hand, he hadn't been concentrating like he needed to. He'd had Montana on his mind much more than he'd wanted, but there didn't seem to be anything he could do about it. Luke liked a challenge. And he wasn't used to being told no. So what was this all about?

He watched as she dismounted from Murdock before he'd fully stopped his gallop. She landed with boot heels planted in the soft dirt and ran a little with him.

"Are you thinking of competing in goat tying?" he drawled, startling her, because she hadn't known he was there. Seeing him, her chin whipped upward.

"Where did you come from? I didn't see you come in." She was breathing a little hard from running alongside her horse.

"I think that's because you were obviously concentrating. That's a good thing, right?"

"Right. But I thought I was alone."

"Sorry. You looked like you were going after a goat."

She shook her head, her eyes flashing with irritation. "Can't do that after college."

"You still looked like that's what you were doing."

She bit the inside of her lip and looked embarrassed. "I used to do that, too. I was, well,

I was seeing if I could still dismount like I used to." She rubbed her palm down the front of her faded jeans.

He grinned. "And you didn't want anybody to see you."

Her brows wrinkled above eyes that would have pinned him to the barn door if they'd gotten any sharper. "I *thought* I was alone."

She was embarrassed—and mad. Her eyes flashed blue-green fire as she looked away from him.

He wondered about that suddenly. It hit him, slammed into him with a force that knocked him back. What was she so mad about?

He stepped forward, drawn to her. Lifting his hand, he touched her cheek. She was breathing hard but didn't move. "What's digging at you?" he asked gently, his thumb tracing her cheek.

Something was there, under the surface eating at her. He sensed it with all of his heart. And he wanted to help. "Tell me what you're so mad about, Montana."

Her heart had stopped beating at the look in Luke's eyes. At the tender touch of his hand and the concern in his voice. "Nothing," she denied, when the turmoil raging inside of her pleaded to be heard. She'd been struggling all morning, having had a phone call from her dad earlier. She hadn't taken the call, but just seeing his name on the ID had upset her.

All the guilt and confused feelings she'd felt Sunday had resurged with a vengeance, and the anger at her dad for causing it all had sent her into a tailspin. Now the uncertainty clung to her once more. The uncertainty of whether she had any forgiveness in her heart. Was it her dad who needed to ask her forgiveness? Then why did she have such guilt hanging over her head about it? After all, wasn't it her dad who'd pretended to be the perfect father, provider, husband?

It was her father who was in the wrong. It was her father who'd made her respect him enough to give up her barrel racing dreams, dreams she'd wanted with all her heart…and it was her father whose lies about who he really was and his betrayal that cut so deep that when she thought about it, the anger tore her up inside.

She didn't think anyone could understand what she was feeling, not even the pastor, not even Lacy—but Luke's questioning gaze blasted through the dark emotions swirling around inside her. It was as if he could see into the deepest corners of her heart, straight to the pain. The very idea set her into action. No, she didn't want him or anyone else seeing that deeply.

She didn't want him knowing how torn up she was. How weak it made her feel. It wasn't his business, and she didn't want to share.

Sharing meant letting him in and she wasn't ready to do that. It was dangerous.

"Nothing is wrong," she repeated, her voice stronger. She stepped back, away from the touch of his hand.

The touch of his dark eyes remained, holding her. His shoulders seemed wide enough to hold her troubles. "I don't believe you," he said. "Something tells me you need a friend. Someone to talk to. Talk to me, Montana."

As if he knew he was onto something. The man was as solid as a redwood, and she wondered how it would feel to be sheltered in his arms. Able to trust again.

"No. It's none of your business," she said. "Leave it be."

"Why? So you can be eaten up by whatever is bothering you. So you can let it get between you and this dream?" He waved toward Murdock.

"Mind your own business," she snapped at him, feeling suddenly ugly inside.

A sudden and devastating smile cracked across his tanned, handsome face. "Sorry, Montana. I've got a feeling that's one request I'm not going to be able to keep."

Montana's heart practically swooned, dipping and tumbling. Shaken by the sincerity in his eyes she did the only thing she could—she spun around and stormed across the arena toward Murdock.

How dare the man try to penetrate the wall she'd built up to protect herself? How weak of her to be tempted to let her defenses down.

Grabbing Murdock's saddle horn, she swung easily onto his back. Feeling like an Indian warrior hitting the warpath, she grabbed the reins, wheeled the poor, startled horse around and galloped him back into the alley. If it hadn't been for the closed gate, she'd have been tempted to keep on riding out of the building.

The worst part about it was Luke knew she was hiding something.

How could a near-total stranger seem to see through her? How?

* * *

He'd hit a nerve. Luke watched the ticked-off cowgirl race out of the alley as though a pack of hungry coyotes were chasing her. She was most definitely stewing about something. Something that cut deep. Something still very raw.

As he watched, she and Murdock flew toward the first barrel. Montana's eyes were zeroed-in on the barrel, but she wasn't in rhythm. They were too fast and she was too close as Murdock started around the barrel.

The sound of her knee connecting with the barrel rang out. The hard impact toppled her from the horse like she'd been shot, and she hit the ground with a thud. Dust flew up around her as she rolled and landed facefirst in the soft dirt.

Luke started running the moment she fell. Skidding to a halt, he gently rolled her over. She blinked, gasped for air, then struggled to sit up. Pain etched her pretty, dirt-streaked face as she grabbed her knee.

"Are you all right?" He could barely hear his stupid question over the pounding of his heart. Of course she wasn't all right. What was he thinking? he wondered as she hugged her knee in pain.

She nodded, but didn't look up at him.

Hurting for her, Luke scooped her into his arms. "Let's get you over here and look at that."

"Put me down," she said, but the tremble in her voice gave away her pain.

"No," he said, holding tight when she struggled against him. "Not till I make sure you're all right." He had a feeling he should do as she demanded—for his own well-being, he should put her down and walk away.

That would be the smart thing to do on his part, but something about Montana Brown brought out the need to dig deeper and find out what had hurt her. Because there was no doubt in his mind that she'd been hurt. And he wanted to help.

Jess would tell him to hit the road and not look back. But he couldn't. For the first time ever, he couldn't walk away.

Montana's knee was still stinging from the direct hit, but it was easing. Being in Luke's arms had sent her reeling. "Not till I make sure you're all right," he'd drawled like John Wayne. Truth be told, if she hadn't been so distracted by being in his arms, she might have thought he was charming!

His arms tightened around her as she struggled to get free of his hold. It was useless, because the man was carrying her firmly toward the benches outside the arena. There was no getting free of him.

"I'm fine." She crossed her arms and tried not to notice how strong he was. *Or* how nice he smelled, a combination of pine and something citrus that drew her to inhale a little deeper. *What was she doing?* A few seconds ago, she was trying to get away from him. Now, she was in his arms…and liking it!

"My knee doesn't hurt anymore." She squirmed for good measure.

"Good. I'm still going to check it out. Be still," he told her, almost harshly as he halted at the bench.

"Why are you here anyway?" she asked, relieved as he lowered her to the first row of the metal grandstand benches.

Sweeping his hat from his head, exposing his dark hair, he went down on one knee and looked her straight in the eyes. Goodness— she was speechless. His dark eyes seemed to burn through her. "Because I wanted to come see what you were doing."

Her pulse skittered at the straightforwardness of his answer. She gulped. "Why would you do that?"

"Because, despite everything, I like you. Does this hurt?" He looked at her knee and gently probed around on it.

Was he kidding? She was feeling no pain at the moment! "It's tender but fine. It won't do you any good to like me. I've told you that." She meant it, too—even if she *had* been tempted to spill her guts to the man only a few minutes ago.

He gave a disbelieving laugh. "Get over yourself, Montana. I thought you and I could be friends. That's all. Whatever it is that's eating at you, you might feel better if you talked about it. *Just* talk."

She studied him, mad at herself because she was tempted. "Why are you so interested in what's eating me?"

"I was right. Something *is* eating at you."

"I didn't say that—"

"Oh, yes, you did."

"Did *not.*"

He dipped his chin, giving her a look that was just plain cute, even if it was a look of disbelief.

He was almost eye level with her, since he was still kneeling and his hand rested on her knee. Her knee that had long since stopped hurting, but was now very aware of his touch.

"Believe me, I know that some things can't be changed." His tone vibrated with sincerity. "But I can tell you that talking does help soften the sting."

That did it, time to move away from the man! Standing abruptly, she took a step away from him, tested her knee and was thankful it felt halfway okay. If she stayed that close to him much longer, she would be in deep trouble.

He stood, too. "It's a wonder your knee didn't swell to the size of a watermelon. And how's your back? I'd give you a score of ten for the dive-and-roll you did when you got tossed."

She laughed, easing the tension. "Amazingly, I'm feeling fine there, too. Of course, that might not be the story when I wake up tomorrow."

"True." He continued watching her as she worked her knee, pacing a little. "Now, do you want to talk about it?"

The man was impossible, she thought, as they stared at each other. She didn't want to tell him her life story. Lacy knew the ridiculous details of her parents' divorce, but she certainly wasn't sharing it with Luke.

Even if he had a way of looking at her as if he understood who she really, really was.

Chapter Seven

"You look like you're moving slow today," Sam said the next morning when Montana limped into the diner. The scent of Sam's mouthwatering breakfast lingered in the air of the rustic diner.

"Yeah," Applegate grunted from the jukebox in the corner. "What happened to you? Get thrown from yor horse?" He grinned and stabbed the music selection he wanted with his boney finger.

"Has somebody been in here talking?" she asked suspiciously.

"Nope," Sam denied. "We didn't need anyone to tell us anything. With you riding like you are and limping like that, too, it ain't rocket science."

"Yup, it shor ain't." App walked to his table and sat down.

"Where's Stanley?" Montana asked. The vacant chair at App's table looked odd.

"He's got the bazooties, ain't nothing more than a bad cold, but he decided he'd better hole up in his house and let it run its course."

"I'm sorry about that." She liked Stanley. Applegate and he might be nosey, but they'd always been sweet to her.

"Me, too. Leaves me without a playin' partner."

Montana held back a chuckle at his sour-faced frown.

"How are you at checkers?" he asked, brightening like a lightbulb at his idea.

"I thought you'd never ask," she grinned, unable to resist plopping down across from him. "Pass me some sunflower seeds, please."

"Really?" His jaw dropped.

She held her hand out. "Oh, yeah, I'm sure. I've been wanting to do this ever since I got to town."

A huge smile lit up across App's face. He handed her the five-pound bag of sunflower seeds and she dug out a small handful. "Is this enough?"

"Might be a few too many. You'll look like a chipmunk if you put too many in."

"I'd watch out if I was you," Sam warned, from the table near the back where a booth full of cowboys were chomping down on breakfast like it was their last meal.

"I'm not afraid of Applegate," she huffed, and tossed the sunflower seeds into her mouth.

He hiked a bushy brow. "You shor about that?"

She rubbed her hands together in anticipation. "Oh, I'm *shor,* all right," she warned. "Show me what you got, dude." This was going to be fun.

She and App studied the board.

"You go first." He squinted at her from across the table, like a gunfighter gauging his opponent. He looked to Montana like he had an itchy trigger finger. Holding her in his sights, he leaned out then one, two, three—he fired several sunflower shells at the spittoon on the floor next to the table.

Feeling like the shells were growing in her mouth she leaned forward and took aim then fired away. Sadly, her shells spurted out kind of sickly like, missing their mark and hitting the floor in silence. Laid there with no glory. It was embarrassing, really.

App hitched a caterpillar eyebrow. "I hope ya play checkers better'n ya spit."

She pushed the shells still in her mouth to the side so she could speak. "I'm going to try. It's been a while, but it's probably like riding a horse."

"Ya think?"

"I think." She winked at the older man, then made the first move. "Game on," she said. It had been a long time since she'd played checkers. Chess had been more her dad's speed. "More of a thinking-man's game," he'd been fond of saying, and had challenged her often. She'd been bored with the game, but she was glad to play it with him. Getting close to her dad had never been easy. Some kids played catch with their dad. She played chess. Not that she'd been very good at it, but she'd tried. She'd always wished they could have gone horseback riding together. The fact that he'd gotten her a horse when she was twelve had been a total surprise. Thinking back on it now, it was also about the time he'd begun to spend more time at the office.

"You gonna move that checker or jest stare it ta death?"

"Oh," she gasped, nearly choking on a shell. She'd zoned out for a minute. "Hold your horses, I'm jumping." She took a jump, and he immediately jumped two of hers.

"You ain't too smart at this here game, are ya?"

Sam shook his head across the room. "I warned ya not ta get involved with ole App thar. He ain't too good of a sport."

The door opened and she glanced over her shoulder. Instantly, she froze. Luke strode inside and his gaze locked onto hers like a missile onto a target. His eyes flicked from her to the room, then back to her.

"Hey thar, Luke," App bellowed. "Get on over here and help a poor old fellow out."

"Whoa, no outside help," Montana growled, staring at the checkerboard, then making her move. She could feel Luke standing there, looking over her shoulder.

"Looks like he's not the one who needs help," he drawled.

She twisted her head and scowled up into his cocoa-colored eyes. He blinked innocently and smiled.

"Don't look at me like that. I'm only sayin' that was a lousy move you just made."

"Well, don't be sayin' then. I'll make my own moves and suffer or celebrate on my own." She spat a sunflower seed at the spittoon, and it hit the edge before landing on his boot. Perfect shot.

The look on his face was priceless. She grinned at him.

"Cute. Real cute." He slid across the floor to stand beside App. "I think I'll watch you suffer from over here."

She wasn't planning on losing, but App made his jump, and after she made her next move, the sly man *wiped* her out! Talk about feeling foolish…it was pitiful. After that, the game was short and not so sweet. It was humiliating. Chess was more complicated, and yet she'd lost to App like a schoolgirl who'd never played a game of chess or checkers.

Eyeing her, App chucked a handful of sunflower seeds into his mouth and grinned, showing teeth all the way back to his molars. "That was like taking candy from a baby."

Luke chuckled. "Those very well could be fighting words, App. Montana doesn't take losing very well."

Sam had stopped by to watch the last play, and now he snorted. "App don't, either. Stanley usually whups him good."

"He does not," App grumbled.

Sam hooted with laughter. "You can deny

it all you want, Applegate Thornton, but you know it's the truth."

"It's all right, App." Montana grinned, feeling at peace with the loss. She'd enjoyed her game despite Luke's presence. Why was it, when she didn't want a man in her life, God sent one along who totally made her crazy?

"Fellas, it's been fun, but I've gotta go," she said.

"But you ain't ate nothin'," Sam said.

"I just came in to say hi. I was picking up a few supplies down at Pete's and thought I'd pop in."

App grinned. "You didn't know you was gonna get yourself talked into a rowdy game of checkers, did ya?"

"No, App. I had no idea I was going to be a stand-in for Stanley. You tell him he better feel better soon, because I'm not doing his empty chair justice."

"I'll tell him. I'm goin' over thar in a few minutes ta take him some chicken noodle soup ole Sam cooked up special fer him."

"You better be careful and not catch his bug."

"I can't catch it. I ain't goin' past the porch. He's on his own from thar on out."

Montana could understand App's attitude.

He really didn't need to catch what his buddy had. But what if Stanley needed someone to check on him more closely? Her immune system was excellent; she hadn't been ill in ages. "What would he say if I took the soup by to him?"

All three men stared at her as if she was the last person on earth they expected to offer such an act of kindness. "Why are y'all looking at me like I just said the last thing any of you expected me to say?"

Sam slapped his white dishrag over his shoulder. "Fer starters, you don't hardly know Stanley."

"I know Stanley. I've been in here several times since I came to town, and he's been nothing but nice to me."

"That is true," App said. "Stanley's loud, but he liked you from the moment you stomped in here with Lacy. 'Sides that, any friend of Lacy's is a friend of ours...and better than that, yor her family."

"That's awful sweet of you to say. I liked the three of you from the first time I met y'all, too." She included Sam in the three. She did not look at Luke on that one.

Sam gave her a frank look. "I kin tell you fer shor that Stanley would prefer gettin' his chicken soup delivered by a purdy gal like you a whole lot more than from a shriveled up old geezer like App. I'll go fix it up right now."

Luke crossed his arms, watching her with an expression that was part amused, part amazed. Did he really not think she could be nice and take a sick man a bowl of soup?

"Do you know where Stanley lives?" Luke asked finally.

"No. But App can give me directions."

"It's kinda off the beaten path," App said. "Stanley lives off a dirt road, off of another dirt road, way down past my house."

"You can tell me. I can follow directions pretty good." Did they really didn't think she couldn't take directions? How hard could it be to find a dirt road?

Sam came out of the kitchen with a large carryout bag. "You jest take this to him and tell him it should last him a couple of days. But if I was you, I'd get ol' Luke here ta drive ya out thar. Ain't no tellin' what in the world you might run into out thar in the boonies."

"Guys, I can take care of myself."

Sam wagged his head. "It ain't got a thang in the world ta do with that. My Adela called me while I was back thar gettin' this ready and I told her you was takin' it out to Stanley and she said I was not to let you go alone. Under no circumstances were you to head out thar without Luke here drivin' you." He dropped his chin. "And if my Adela tells me that, then that's what I aim ta tell you."

Montana would have protested and done exactly what she wanted. However, she glanced over at Luke, who gave her a what-are-you-afraid-of look. What *was* she afraid of? Nothing. She wasn't scared of him. She could let him drive her out there and it made no difference to her.

"Load up then. What are we waiting on?" Taking the soup, she headed toward the door. When she got there, she turned and gave App and Sam warning looks. "But you two better not make anything out of this little trip, other than me letting Luke take me out to Stanley's."

Two sets of bushy brows rose to meet thinning hairlines despite both men trying their hardest to look innocent. She almost laughed, but one glance up at Luke and she scowled instead. The man was simply too good-looking for his own good. Okay, the man was too good-looking for *her* good. As he held the door open for her and she squeezed past him with the bag of soup, she reminded herself that she wasn't supposed to be thinking about how good he smelled, how good he looked or how nice he was going along with two old men with matchmaking on their minds.

"It's nice of you to take this out to Stanley." Luke held the door of his truck open for Montana, and just naturally took her elbow to help her up into the seat.

"It's the right thing to do."

He liked that, he thought, as he closed the door and headed around to his side. He glanced toward the diner's big window and there stood Sam beside App's table. Both men were grinning like two kids thinking they were pulling a good one. He chuckled as he got behind the wheel.

"They think they're so sneaky. Do you believe the story about Miss Adela calling?" Montana asked.

Luke started the truck and backed out before he answered. He wanted to get away from prying eyes. He had seen a few other eyes staring out windows, too. From over at the candy store. And he thought he'd seen Esther Mae looking out of Ashby's Treasures—the ladies' clothing store that was directly across the street from Sam's diner. Everyone in town would know about this little trip before they even made it out to Stanley's.

"It sounded like something she might say, so it could be true. If not, Sam's getting pretty creative, isn't he?"

She laughed at that. "Oh, yes, he is. So, is Stanley's place really that hard to find?"

"Oh, yeah. The man lives down by the river, and you have to drive halfway across Texas as the crow flies to get there." He grinned at her. "You'll see. And you'll be glad you decided not to be scared of me and let me drive you."

"I wasn't scared of you."

"Yeah, you were. Are."

She shot him a glare that would have stopped a raging bull in its tracks. He challenged her with his expression before turning back to the road. Even ornery, she interested him. He wondered what it was that had her so mad and tense half the time. He aimed to find out, just like he aimed to get her to go out with him. He liked a challenge, and if there was one thing about Montana Brown that was as clear as the blue sky in front of them, it was that she was a challenge.

He sometimes wondered how his life would be if God hadn't created him to be as stubborn as he was, and as determined to meet a challenge head-on. Jess and Colt always called him bullheaded, but it was his bullheadedness that had helped them all cope whenever their parents were yelling and screaming at each other back when they were younger. He'd only been ten when the worst fights were going on. When his poor mother was at her wit's end and just barely coping with the struggles of being married to his alcoholic dad. He'd been old enough to know he needed to get his brothers out of the house. They'd end up out in the neighbor's big barn, down the dirt road where they lived. Or they'd go fishing in the pond around the corner.

He'd been fourteen when his parents had finally split. And his mom left him to be in charge of his dad—and his brothers. She'd left him there. Nothing had ever been, or would be, harder than that day. He still had a hard time thinking about it. His brothers did, too, especially Jess.

"So, how's it going out at Lacy's?" he asked a few miles down the road, after the silence had stretched about as long and tight as it could go.

"Great."

He turned onto the first dirt road of many connecting ones, then he gave her a long stare. "That's it? That's the extent of our conversation?" She looked at him and her lips lifted into a half grin that did funny things to his insides.

"I guess ignoring you isn't going to work, is it?"

"Or be very nice."

She laughed. "No, I guess it wouldn't be that, either."

"It does tend to take a lot of effort to be rude," he said. She turned slightly in her seat, so that she was facing him. He kept his eyes on the road.

"This is very true. It can be exhausting when the man can't take a hint."

It was his turn to chuckle. "I'm stubborn that way."

"I've figured that out. But so am I. I'm just giving in because I need all my energy to compete with Murdock. Poor horse is giving me two hundred percent, so I have to try to give him at least a measly little one hundred. I have enough things stealing energy from my concentration without being rude to you, too."

"You're honest, I'll give you that."

"I'm *very* honest. Riding the fence hasn't ever been one of my strong points. At least not usually."

"I have you figured to ride it when you don't have options." He wasn't sure where this conversation had come from, but he knew they were hitting close to home on something. Her sudden thoughtfulness made him certain of it. She looked straight ahead, chewing her lip. Something was going on inside that head of hers, and for some reason he was eaten up with wanting to know what it was. He shouldn't want to, but there was no way of denying the truth. He wanted to know what made Montana Brown tick.

"You have a lot on your mind?" It was as much a statement as a question. He'd let her take it whichever way she wanted to.

She blinked and her troubled eyes cleared. "Yes. Doesn't everyone?"

"Yes, frankly. But sometimes, it helps to talk about it. Do you need an objective point of view?"

"Are you always so nosy, Mr. Holden? If so, this may be why you can't hold a date."

"Hey, I hold a date as long as I want."

"Yes, you keep reminding me of that unflattering fact about yourself."

"I'm not always this nosy," he growled, choosing to ignore her comments. There was obviously no changing her view on his personal life. They'd reached a fork in the road, with a third dirt road feeding off of one of the forks. It was the third road that he took. From here on, the road would get more rutted. Stanley really needed to get the county to come out and grade the thing. If the river was to suddenly rise, he'd be cut off. That wasn't good.

"Why me? Why do you want to poke around in my business?"

Man, the woman had a way of putting things. "I want to know why you're always this angry. I want to help. Believe it or not, I know what it's like to walk around eaten up with anger."

"I'm not always like this. And you don't know how much I wish I wasn't. But there are just some things in this world a person can't change. Some folks are just going to disappoint us."

"Now, *that* I know something about." He wished he didn't. "Sometimes you just have to learn not to expect too much out of people. Sad but true."

Anger crossed her expression, her eyes flashed as she crossed her arms and shook her head. "That's just a sorry excuse. I want people to expect a lot out of me. I want people to know that I'm who I say I am. Others should, too."

He could feel her pain. What had caused it? Stanley's house came into view up ahead, and Luke wished he lived about ten more miles down the road. He gave the only advice he believed in. "Then be that person, but don't expect it from others. You only control your standards."

"Is that what you do? How you live your life?"

He pulled to a stop in Stanley's yard. "To a point. I mean, I know that here in Mule Hollow, there are plenty of folks who'd come through for me in a heartbeat. But still, let's just say, when you're raised to expect the worst from those who're supposed to care for you—there is always a part of you that expects the worst from everyone."

Looking straight at each other, neither one of them moved. The ebb and flow of a pulsing tension connected them. He felt the connection and knew she did, too.

She finally gave a nod.

"I guess that's one reason I wanted to bring Stanley his soup."

The tension eased. "And I guess that's one reason I wanted to come along. Like you said, it's the right thing to do."

Some of the trouble in her eyes wasted away, replaced with a little sparkle. "You are just full of surprises."

He wanted to press for more, but the teasing banter was a good thing. He liked it. "It's about time I got a little love."

She laughed and opened her door. "Oh, don't get a big head now. I wouldn't go that far. Not by a long shot."

Chapter Eight

Poor Stanley! When he opened the door, his plump face was pale, his cheeks extra pink and his nose was a bright, rosy red. "I hate to say it, but you look terrible, Stanley."

That got Montana a smile despite his ill looks. "I feel tur-rable, too," he said. "What are y'all doin' here?"

She held up the bag of soup. "Didn't you hear? Sam has hired us out as his new delivery crew. You're our first client. Between you and me, this character they have drivin' me is a bit shady. I think I was hired on to keep him from scaring old ladies."

Stanley coughed, long and hard, but grinned and nodded as he put a tissue up to his red nose. "He sure looks like a character, all right," he managed.

"Cut it out, you two or I'm about to get insulted. I drove all the way out here to rescue you with soup, Stanley. *And* to keep *you* from getting lost in the boonies and causing half of the county to come out and search for you, Montana. The phrase is 'thank you very much.'"

His drawl was cute, Montana thought as she rolled her eyes and looked at Stanley in the doorway. He was leaning against the door, looking weak. "He's a big baby, if you didn't already know that. Just what I don't like about a man. Always whining." She was enjoying this, and Luke was being so nice playing along, helping to lift Stanley's spirits.

Stanley battled another fit of coughing. "Need ta watch out fer the likes of him. I'd invite y'all in, but you might catch whatever I've got that's kicking my rump." He frowned, held on to the door frame and wheezed, "And that wouldn't be good." He held his hand out for the soup.

Montana held tightly on to the bag. "Nope, not leaving," she said breezily, and scooted past him into the house. "I'm going to sit you down somewhere comfortable before you fall down. Then I'm going to warm this up for you."

Luke followed her in, despite the look of

dismay on Stanley's lovable face. Set on getting her way on this, she saw the edge of the counter through a doorway and headed that way.

"But you might get sick," Stanley protested, padding along behind her in his stocking feet.

"And we might not." She stopped in her tracks at the kitchen door—oh, what a mess! The poor man probably hadn't washed a dish since he started feeling bad. It was apparent. He'd probably barely felt like figuring out *what* to eat. Turning around, she pointed at Luke. "Could you take him into the den and help him get comfortable? I'll have this heated up in a jiffy. Then I'm going to clean this kitchen while you keep him company as he eats. A little conversation might make you feel better, Stanley."

"Aw, y'all don't have ta go ta all that trouble."

"Are you kidding?" Montana grimaced. "I had to play checkers with App this morning. It was horrible. You've got to get better so you can go back in there and defend me. He tore me up."

"No way," Stanley grunted.

"Oh, it's true," Luke joined in. "I witnessed

it. Montana can ride a horse like greased lightning, but at checkers, believe me, she stinks."

"That's turr-able." *Cough.* "Jest turr-able."

"Not as terrible as it's going to be when you play him again and whup him in my defense. Soup and a clean kitchen in trade for a little good ol'-fashioned payback. How's that sound?"

"I kin do that," Stanley agreed, already walking into the den. She could see his recliner and quilt waiting for him. "Sounds like I get the easy end of this deal." He paused to cough, his shoulders shaking before he trudged forward and made it to the chair.

Setting the package of soup on the counter, Montana went in search of a clean bowl. This had certainly not been the morning she'd envisioned when she'd headed into town for feed for Murdock. As she waited for the soup to heat in the microwave, she began scrubbing dishes to go in the dishwasher. It was a really good feeling, to know she was doing something good. If she did get sick, it was going to be well worth it.

She thought of Luke's teasing and the smile he'd given her just now. Getting sick could definitely have its positives if he brought *her* some soup. One thing she was realizing about Luke was that he was a giving person. He had work to do, but he'd taken time out and come along with her. It was sweet.

He was sweet. She paused scrubbing the dish in her hands—Luke had his good side, it was a fact. She sighed…whupped, on that count.

There was simply no way to deny it.

Even if she wanted to!

By the expression on her face, Montana gauged Norma Sue's mood to be jolly. More like ecstatic. Her smile was practically stretched from ear to ear as she strode into the arena the day after Montana and Luke had gone to see Stanley. Word was out just like she knew it would be.

People were talking. The matchmakers, that is, and Montana had set herself up for it like a crazy fool. Trailing behind the grinning cattlewoman was Esther Mae. She was beaming brighter than her red hair, and her eyes were twinkling so brightly, with the sheer pleasure of the hunt, that Montana knew she was in trouble. Behind both of them trailed Adela, looking for all the world like a woman who knew a secret.

She might have messed up. Really. She'd gotten so caught up in trying not to let Luke bother her, she'd taken up the challenge and let Luke drive her out to Stanley's place. Now she was going to have to pay the consequences.

Even if there was no truth to what they thought was a blossoming romance, the seed was planted. "Romance, ha!" she muttered to Murdock as she leaned down to pat his neck. "Me and that man would drive each other crazy." *But you didn't yesterday. You enjoyed helping Stanley with him.*

"What are y'all ladies doing out here?" she asked, ignoring the voice in her head as she loped Murdock over to the fence.

Esther Mae fanned herself with her hand. "We've come to make sure the concession stand is in order for the crowds in two weeks."

"We wouldn't want everyone to get here and not be able to buy a soda and some popcorn." Norma Sue stuck her hand through the fence and scratched Murdock's chin.

"How are you today, dear?" Adela asked, her smile warming Montana, despite knowing she was about to get the third degree.

"I'm great. We're coming along better

every day. Murdock's not quite so upset with me lately."

"Well, that's wonderful," Esther Mae gushed. She wore a pair of bright pink pants and a white shirt with a huge, sparkly pink rose on it. She looked as cheerful and happy as any woman Montana had ever met. "That was such a nice thing you did yesterday, taking soup out to poor Stanley. And Luke was such a gentleman to drive you. That Stanley, he lives too far out in the sticks for a young woman like you to travel there all by herself. I'm glad the fellas were smart enough to send along Luke."

"I thought Adela suggested Luke drive me?" Montana watched Adela's blue eyes widen in surprise.

"Me?" Adela placed a delicate hand to her cheek. "Well, um, those men must have thought you might listen to my advice. I'll have to say something to Sam about that."

"It's fine." Montana chuckled. "He said you'd called—"

"I did call. And he did tell me what you were doing. I did say that it would be nice if Luke drove you, but that was after Sam said he was going to get Luke to take you."

"I didn't mind," Montana said. "And Stanley's place was way out in the boondocks. Oh, my word—if I'd have taken a wrong turn, there's no telling where I'd be right now."

"Ain't that the truth," Norma Sue grunted.

"What about that Luke?" Esther Mae beamed, stepping closer, her eyes wide with enthusiasm. "Y'all had a good time didn't y'all? He's such a cutie-patootie!"

Montana almost choked. "Does he know you call him that?"

"Why don't you call him up and tell him? I don't mind. You could call him a few names yourself while you're on the phone…sugar pie, honeybunches, sweetheart."

"That's okay, we'll let it slide this time."

"You could go out with the poor ol' cowboy—"

"Norma Sue, I am *not* interested. Honestly, how many women has he been out with this year?" Did they not get that the man took nothing serious about a relationship? A relationship—when she did decide to have one—would be a very serious commitment. A man had to take it seriously, too, and be loyal—obviously something her dad knew nothing about.

"He's been out with a few," Norma Sue

said apologetically. "He just needs the right one to come along and make him want to get to know you a little better."

"But I don't *want* to get to know him better."

Esther Mae frowned. "You are young and pretty, and need to be doing more than holing up with a horse and a baby. I love baby Tate with all my heart, but Lacy and Clint don't want you spending all your time babysitting. Everyone needs a night out. And I know you've got dreams and goals and all, but this horse is not going to keep you warm at night, and hold your hand when you get old and gray like us. Not that I'm gray-headed like Norma Sue here, but you know what I'm talking about."

Norma Sue was looking at Esther Mae like she'd lost her marbles. "You know good and well that beneath that red dye your natural red has disappeared. For all you know, you might be as white-headed as Adela!"

"No offense, Adela, but I am not that white-headed. Thank you very much," she huffed and fussily patted her flaming red hair.

Montana enjoyed the three ladies' teasing for a few more moments. She wondered if they would leave without checking the concession stand, which had been their ruse for coming to hound her about Luke. It would be funny if they did. Oddly, as much as she didn't want to be set up by the posse, it was fun to see them in action.

"I love babysitting Tate," she said in the baby's defense. "As a matter of fact, I'm watching him tonight so Lacy and Clint can go to the movies and out to eat in Ranger. This is the anniversary of the day she first came to town and met him."

"Oh, what a day that was!" Esther Mae exclaimed.

"It was a true blessing," Adela added.

Norma Sue pulled her hand away from Murdock and stuffed it into her overalls pocket. "And they are a perfect match. We did good, helping out with that, if I may say so myself."

Lacy and Clint were perfect for each other and Montana was so happy for them both. But she was content to not join the married mix. If only the ladies could understand that. She didn't let herself consider that she might be unfair to Luke. The niggling thought hovered at the edge of her conscience, though.

She was relieved a good while later when

the posse left. After they had, in fact, made a trip inside the concession stand. She wasn't sure if they got what they were after, but she was relieved to see them go.

The rest of the afternoon as she and Murdock practiced, men tramped in and out of the arena area, working on various areas of the building. She wondered if Luke might show up, and found herself watching for him. After all, it was his animals going into the pens that were being worked on.

She spent the rest of the afternoon looking toward the entrance more times than she wanted to count.

Luke did not show up.

When she finally took Murdock to his stall and brushed him down before turning him out to relax in the outside lot, she berated herself for letting her thoughts dwell on Luke the entire time. True, she wasn't interested in the man. But still, she felt a hum of expectation when he was around. In addition to a *very* loud hum of irritation.

She watched Murdock nibble grass and lazily enjoy his freedom.

For the first time in her life, she, too, was experiencing her freedom. Freedom from her father's and mother's expectations. Freedom from worrying about pleasing them. And freedom from the guilt they'd made her feel when she wanted to do things her way. When did a girl become a woman who could make her own choices? When was a woman able to go her own way and decide her life on her own terms?

These had been the questions plaguing her while growing up and longing to hone her talent and see if she could make it as a professional barrel racer. She'd felt she'd had the talent to make it into the money, to gain sponsorships and to provide for herself with a lifestyle she'd dreamed of. But she'd honored her father's and mother's wishes. She'd set her dreams aside and become an accountant, then entered the family firm. There was nothing wrong with being an accountant—but she hadn't chosen it for herself. Her father had said it was a respectable, well-paying career for a woman. And so she'd become one. She'd put on her business suit and stowed her boots and jeans, along with her dreams. As she'd picked up her calculator she left Murdock to while away in a pasture, his unbelievable talent wasted.

Freedom. She had it now, but oddly, it came at a high price. Her father's betrayal and her mother's betrayal by living the lie and not telling Montana what was going on had done the thing she'd longed for all her life. It had given her the freedom to feel no guilt over choosing her own way. And here she was, living life on her terms and loving it.

Despite the heartache that brought her here, she did love it. The idea struck Montana as gently as the breeze that whispered across her skin.

She loved her life right now.

And if there was a niggling feeling of guilt over not being able to forgive her dad for lying to her. For betraying her mother. And being such a hypocrite about being so respectable, when in fact, he was so *not* respectable in his behavior. If there was any guilt at all over any of that, then she was learning to live with it.

Turning to head to the house and her date with a darling boy named Tate, she breathed deeply of the fresh, pine-laced air and let the joy of her freedom take hold. She was happy.

Yes, she was still angry, and she had her moments where the anger snuck up and ate her up, but it was getting easier each day to ignore it.

She opened the back door to the house and walked inside, choosing to acknowledge the denial.

Denial meant freedom. And that denial didn't need a man complicating it and messing it up.

Chapter Nine

"So you're sure that you're going to be all right with us going out?"

Montana bounced Tate on her hip, making him giggle. "Are you kidding? Me and Tater can't wait to have the house to ourselves. We plan on having a party. He's got all his buddies hiding in the bushes, waiting to see y'all's taillights disappearing down the drive. Isn't that right, little buddy?"

Clint wrapped his arms around Lacy from behind and grinned at Montana. "You and the kiddo have fun, then. I'm taking my wife out on the town. If the party gets too rowdy, call the cops. Brady or Zane will come to the rescue."

"Or you could call Luke," Lacy added innocently. "Word has it that it's only a matter of time before the matchmakers have you two tied up tighter than a—"

Montana threw Tate's stuffed puppy at her, hitting Lacy in the chin. "You are really pushing it, cuz."

Lacy laughed, walking over to kiss her baby goodbye. "You know I love you. But seriously, they *have* targeted you."

"And you haven't?"

"Well, no. Now, why would I do that when I know you aren't interested?"

Clint rolled his eyes and cleared his throat loudly.

"Don't worry, Clint, I'm not buying her innocent act, either."

"Then fine. You know that I want you to relax and get on with your life. But I also want you to think about what God has in store for you, and we both know that there is something going on between you and that handsome cowboy."

"Maybe it has nothing whatsoever to do with God."

"*Maybe* not," Lacy said. "But maybe it does."

"Luke's a good guy, Montana," Clint said, serious now. "He had a rough upbringing. Not your typical happy family. Not even your *almost* happy family. He worked here on the ranch beside me after they moved here growing up, and he idolized my dad. He's a quick learner and as reliable as they come. But he's never, ever talked about marriage. So, in that respect, you two match up. As a guy, I'll tell you he might be one who never marries. Though I know he's building a ranch he can pass on. He's setting down roots that will last and become a legacy." He hunched his shoulders and tilted his head. "The matchmakers may be wrong about him—and his brothers Jess and Colt. Some men aren't married because they just aren't ready and haven't met the right woman. And then there are some who got such a bad taste growing up that it's not a place they want to return. That said, I for one can tell him that, when God puts the right woman in his path, there is nothing on earth that can compare to the fullness life takes on from there. That goes for you, too."

Montana was shocked by such a long speech from Clint, as much as the words he spoke about Luke. "Thanks, both of you. I'm touched by your concern. I know you both mean well, and it means a lot to me. You will never, ever know how much. Luke and I will be just fine. For starters, we do understand each other, so it's good. Now go, have a good time." She waved them toward the door. "Tater's little buddies are probably sucking their thumbs fast asleep under the mesquite bushes by now."

Montana was watching Tate show off his new crawling skills when a truck pulled up in front of the house. She wasn't expecting anyone, she realized as she headed toward the door. Through the big windows, she saw Luke step out of the truck, hesitate, then slam the door and stride her way. The rush of pleasure at his appearance surprised her. All afternoon, she'd looked forward to his showing up in the barn, and the disappointment hadn't been something she wanted to think about. Now a glimpse of him in a chocolate-brown button-up shirt that matched his eyes had her pulse bouncing off the charts.

She pulled the door open before he knocked, startling him. "A little late to be checking on the arena setup, isn't it?"

"I didn't come for that." He looked past her into the house.

Following his gaze, she glanced over her shoulder to see Tate rise up on wobbly knees and reach toward the coffee table. "Oh, no, you don't." She laughed, hurrying back to the tot. "Come on in," she called, catching Tate just in time to keep him from bumping his tiny chin. Swinging him into her arms, she kissed his cheek as she turned back toward her unexpected guest. "Clint's not here. He and Lacy went on a date."

He looked puzzled as he scanned the room. "A date? But—where's everyone else?"

"Who?" Now it was her turn to look puzzled.

"I saw Norma Sue at the feed store and she asked me to come to a rodeo committee meeting here at seven."

Montana laughed. She couldn't help it. The sneaky Norma Sue. "You've been had. You know that, don't you?"

"I should have known." He gave a short laugh, snugged his hat tighter to his head, in a movement that spoke of embarrassment. "I've watched those women in action over and over again, and they *still* got one over on me."

"They knew I was going to be watching Tate tonight. They came poking around earlier, when I was riding." She tried to figure out what to do next. Did she ask him to stay? Did she want him to go? It was one weird situation she found herself in. Shifting Tate in her arms, she used him as a sort of emotional shield between the two of them. Something to keep her from thinking about hugging the man or kissing him.

She held Tate tighter as Luke walked toward the kitchen. "So, do you have anything to eat?"

"I might, but I don't remember inviting you to stay."

He shrugged one muscled shoulder and hooked a thumb in his pocket as he studied her. He looked as if he could care less whether he stayed or not. It had her insides feeling queasy. Was that romance in the air, or just butterflies in her stomach at the thought of wondering such a thing? She didn't want romance. She didn't want the hint of it. Did she?

"There's roast beef in the fridge, and potatoes," she heard herself say.

"You sit and I'll fix it."

Her mouth dropped. "I didn't invite you to stay for dinner."

"So?"

She looked at Tate. "Did you hear that, Tate? This is not the way to act. He—" she nodded her head toward the unbelievably good-looking man in her kitchen "—has a lot to learn in the romance department."

"Who said anything about romance? I'm just having dinner. The way I figure it, if you won't go out with me for dinner, then I come to you. I owe the posse for this one."

"But I haven't told you that you could stay yet."

He opened the door to the fridge and studied the contents in silence. Acting like he didn't need her invitation, he pulled the pot from the shelf and set it on the counter. "This looks good."

Yes, it did. The cowboy had skills, she thought, as he began opening drawers and finding the items he needed: forks, knives, glasses. She cuddled Tate and watched in silence while Luke made himself at home in Lacy's kitchen. It amused her that he didn't ask. That he just did it.

He was taking charge…and oddly enough she liked it. It was flattering that he wanted to have dinner with her this much. She admired his never-give-up mentality.

"Lacy and Clint seem really happy," he said at last while he was ladling roast and gravy onto plates and nuking them in the microwave.

"Romance is alive and well at the Matlock house."

Luke leaned against the counter, hooked his thumb in his jeans pocket and held her gaze. "Do you ever wish that for yourself?"

"You've come into the house, invited yourself to dinner and now you're asking some *very* personal questions. I'm not too sure I want to play this game."

He hiked a shoulder. "I'm just curious. I ask everyone the same question—well, sort of."

"Ah, yes, the no-strings-attached question. And here I thought you were about to ask me to marry you."

"Not today. So *do* you?"

"Persistent little badger, aren't you?"

"Yes. And I'd rather be called something a little more masculine than a badger. You sure know how to knock a man's ego down a notch."

She laughed full and hard at that. Tate grinned and clapped his hands. Luke laughed at them, sending a ripple of awareness through Montana. His smile faded suddenly, as something passed between them.

Same as she'd felt that day in the arena when he'd tried to get her to talk to him, she felt drawn to Luke. It was unmistakable.

She admitted it. Admitted to herself that she liked him. She liked his blunt manner and his frank openness about what he wanted out of life. The man was truthful when it came to his expectations. At least it appeared so. When a woman went out with the guy, it was with eyes wide-open, because he'd made himself clear. Honesty was a good thing. Montana had felt bad for tea-tossing Erica that night at Lacy's barbecue. Now that she really understood Luke, she realized that tea tosser had to have understood the reality—Luke wasn't looking for marriage, and just the mention of it had him throwing on the brakes.

"I think I owe you an apology," Montana said.

"You talkin' to me?" he asked, spinning from where he'd just closed the door to the microwave, a look of mock disbelief on his face, his hand to his heart. "Say it ain't so, Sally. What in the world for?"

"The man is crazy," she said to Tate. "My name isn't Sally. Is yours?" Tate grinned at her and tried to pull her hair. "Maybe you didn't deserve to have tea poured all over you the other night."

"Now that is interesting. Very interesting. How did you come up with that deduction, Sherlock?"

She cocked her head to the side. "You make yourself very clear about you not being a marrying man. Tea tosser had to have known that, or you slipped up."

"I didn't slip up."

"Didn't think so. Anyway, I'm sorry I was so hard on you. But I still don't want to date you."

"And yet, here we are having dinner at Lacy's. Together. No date intended."

"Well, there you go. That fixes both our dilemmas." Not exactly, since it was a setup by the matchmakers, but she'd go along with it.

"If that's settled, then let's eat. I'm starving."

She'd have fixed Tate something, but he'd already had his bottle. Instead, she walked across the large living room and set him down in his playpen. Handing him his favorite teething ring and plush toy, she then headed back to the kitchen. Her pulse skipped like a dozen pebbles skimming over water as she watched Luke. They were having dinner. Sucking in a deep breath, she tried to relax. Luke had set the plates, napkins and flatware out, and was filling glasses with tea as she sat down.

"I figured you wouldn't toss this on me."

"I'll behave. I promise."

He placed the glasses on the counter next to their plates, then sat down beside her on a stool. Montana wondered if, by sitting at the kitchen island instead of the table, he thought she'd feel more inclined to believe this wasn't a date.

It *wasn't* a date, but the posse would never believe it.

"Earlier, I was teasing Lacy and Clint that Tate's little buddies were hiding outside in the bushes waiting for them to leave so they could come inside and play with Tate. But it's actually the posse who's probably out there. I can see them in the bushes wearing camouflaged outfits with mud swiped under their eyes, believing that we're on a date."

His eyes danced. "Right. I can almost hear the sound of their chatter."

He picked up a glass of tea and held it up

in salute. "Let them have their fun. We understand each other. Agreed?"

Smiling, she picked her glass up and touched it to his. "Agreed."

Chapter Ten

ᕗ

They made small talk over dinner. Montana knew, from the day in the arena, that Luke was curious about her and she was curious about him and his past. But he didn't ask her and she didn't ask him. She was fighting through her issues on her own, and knew that, though he'd tempted her a couple of times with his strong shoulder to cry on, she was *not* going to go there.

It didn't matter how many times those deep, dark eyes of his called out to her to spill her guts to him.

Instead, they filled the blank space with small talk that led to stories about Luke's friends who had been targeted by the matchmaking posse and lost. His smile was warm and teasing when he said *lost*. They both understood what that meant.

There had been rumors of emptied gas tanks, wild hog encounters, help from a matchmaking donkey, which he promised to introduce her to at the festival. Samantha would be the main attraction of the petting zoo.

"It's never totally clear how much of a hand the gals have in all the matches," he said halfway through the roast beef. "But no matter what, we all know they're in the background, pushing love buttons to get whoever they've decided to match up together."

She had a feeling there were several women wishing the matchmakers' button-pushing had included them and Luke. Erica was at the front of the line. "Lacy says they get a lot of help from above."

"I suspect she's right. The matches seem to be good ones. Tate looks like proof to me."

Montana laid her fork down and glanced over at Tate, who'd conked out. He looked so peaceful. "Sadly, kids don't always prove a couple's happiness. Don't get me wrong, I believe Lacy and Clint were a match made in heaven. They didn't have to have Tate to prove it, but I know what you mean." Why, oh, why, had she just done that—opened her big mouth?

Her words had instantly drawn that look back into his eyes, and they were seeking as they settled on her. "I understand that more than you can know. Children don't always mean all is well on the homefront. Wasn't anywhere near right when it came to my home. But then I guess nothing on earth is perfect."

Silence stretched between them for a few moments. Montana held back voicing all the thoughts in her head, because it was just so personal. Still, she wondered about Luke's childhood. The way her thoughts kept swinging over to such a topic was a far cry from the distance she claimed she wanted to keep.

How could it be that she was so put off about the idea of a man in her life, and yet she couldn't seem to stop thinking about Luke and being interested in his past?

He leaned back in his chair. "My thought is that if God isn't in it, then marriage shouldn't be an option."

She was wading into the deep end, and she knew it. "Again, something we agree on."

"What's got you so adamant about that?"

She considered changing the subject, staring into his dark eyes. But the words wanted out too much and she couldn't hold them back. She felt too compelled to say something. "Growing up, I thought my parents had the perfect marriage. They never fought—they didn't really spend time together, but I never thought much about that. In my mind, they'd be together for all time. It's a major blow when you find out your parents are getting divorced. Or that your dad was having an affair." She shook her head. "It's just crazy. Disappointing…pointless, really…" Her voice trailed off and she didn't finish, as she felt the hard nudge of anger try to surface.

He gave her a gentle smile. "Is that what has you so angry?" he asked cautiously, as if afraid she was going to run out of the house and throw herself against a barrel again.

The very idea almost made her chuckle, and in a weird way lifted her up. She sighed. "You know…I can't—" She shook her head slightly, realizing she didn't want to mess up the evening by talking about her troubled past.

"I guess it can go both ways when it comes looking from the inside out," Luke began. "My parents were loud and fought over everything. They made no pretense about not enjoying each other's company. I've never been able to figure out why they were to-gether in the first place. But they were. At least until my mom left when I was about twelve—not sure I blamed her. My dad was a drunk who couldn't hold a job. Worse, he didn't want to hold a job. He wanted every-one else to do the work."

"Your mom left?"

He nodded.

Surely she misunderstood. "Left you with your dad?" Did he mean his mother had left her three small sons with a man who drank and didn't work? He nodded again, and she felt ill. "How did y'all survive?"

"We worked. Me and my brothers."

Though he said the words in a matter-of-fact tone, Montana got a sharp image of Luke and his brothers working at young ages doing any jobs they could find to help support their family. She'd heard the edge to his words, and she studied him. He'd done what he'd had to do to survive. Luke had started overcom-ing challenges early. He'd learned to accept life as a challenge and to want to overcome it.

She was amazed by him. And she admired him. Talk about a complete turnabout on her part.

"How old were you when you started working?" she asked.

"About ten—if you count small odd jobs I did for people. It was good for me. There's nothing wrong with working. We—my brothers and me, are good at that."

"I bet you were. Are."

He gave a small grunt of a laugh. "Yeah, Jess and Colt say we were due for retirement by the time we were in high school."

She chuckled. "I guess that's one way to look at it."

He gave that shrug that she'd come to learn was his. No big deal, it said. "You do what you have to do. We're the men we are today because of the kind of man my dad was. He was the worst role model around, and frankly, I could be bitter about it. And I've had my moments, believe me. But—" he gave an assuring look "—we've made peace with our childhoods. All three of us, in our own way. We each know what we don't want to be—my dad drank himself into an early grave. I couldn't do anything about that. Mac Matlock opened the Bible and showed me Galatians 6:4. It says. 'Each one should test his own actions. Then he can take pride in

himself, without comparing himself to somebody else.'"

He rubbed his thumb along the edge of the
granite counter and studied it as he did it.
"That's what I'm trying to do."

Montana didn't have the words. She was
trying to process all he'd said when he
reached for the plates and stood up, as if
needing to move.

"Those are strong words," she said. "You
are doing great."

"I'm trying. My mother married a couple
more times, then decided to give it up. She
lives in Fredericksburg and manages a small
restaurant. She loves her life now, and that's
important to us. We tried to talk her into
moving out here, when we bought the ranch
last year, but she wouldn't hear of it. She has
her church family there that she's involved
in. She wouldn't budge."

Placing her elbow on the counter and her
chin in her hand, Montana marveled at his attitude. His mother had left him in charge of
his two younger brothers *and* a drunk dad,
and yet he was acting as though nothing out
of the ordinary had happened. Wasn't he
angry at her?

She was angry for him.

What kind of woman did that? She'd left her boys to fend for themselves, and now Luke was talking as if they were best friends.

It was hard to swallow, especially in light of what was happening with her dad. She reached for the collar of her shirt, feeling hot suddenly. Galatians 6:4 played in her head. It said test her own actions…

Her hand trembled slightly as she thought about that. She had to change the subject before she said something she would regret. He had moved on with no anger—she was moving on, too, but she couldn't lose the anger. Not yet, anyway.

"Can I ask you something?" She got up and went to help clear the dishes away, hoping it would help her calm down.

"Sure," he said, opening the dishwasher.

"If you and your brothers have a need to own this ranch so you'll have a legacy for your families, why aren't any of you married?"

He placed a glass in the dishwasher.

"I figure Jess and Colt just haven't met their matches yet. Sure, I want to leave a legacy, but for me that includes helping Colt and Jess build theirs for their family. I'm not getting sidetracked until I do that. My brothers will fall in love, and I'm determined that this ranch will be something they can be proud of when that happens. That's my legacy."

It suddenly made sense. He was the protector. His mother had left him in charge of Colt and Jess, and he was doing that. It didn't matter that they were strong, capable men; this was a challenge he'd accepted, and he was seeing it through. He was taking pride in himself, like the verse said.

Focused. That's what he was, just like she was focusing on her riding. But he was also thinking about God's direction in his life, too. She was more amazed by him with every moment that passed. "We're a lot alike, it seems, Luke Holden." Not exactly, but sort of—what was she saying? She'd handed him the emptied glasses. He took them and his fingers brushed hers. His touch sent her pulse skittering. They were standing close enough for her to see the light flicker in the depths of his eyes.

"How's that?" he asked, his voice smooth as he held her gaze.

Thoughts of his arms around her slammed into her. "We…we're alike—" Her mind went totally blank and she had no clue what she'd been about to say.

He cocked a brow ever so slightly, and one corner of his lips turned up. "We're both focused," he prompted. "And we know what we want."

Yes, that was true. She leaned against the counter and he did the same, his arm touching hers as he watched her, amusement lighting his eyes. Her heart suddenly was pounding inside her chest, and there was a flutter of butterflies in her stomach. "Yes, that's right," she managed. Did she truly know what she wanted? Looking at Luke, she seemed to forget for a minute.

"Are you all right?" he asked, leaning closer, her heart thumping like a rabbit's foot.

In the other room, Tate stirred and whimpered. The sound was like an ice chest of cold water being dumped on her head. She snapped to attention and immediately put distance between them.

"Gotta check on Tater Man!" As if on cue, he started crying. Scooping him up she hugged him to her—unceremoniously, using him as a shield again as she turned back to Luke. He had stopped at the edge of the large area rug. He looked about as uncomfortable as she was—she had a feeling he'd felt exactly what she'd been feeling. There was no way to kid themselves that they weren't attracted to each other. But that was all it was. Attraction. Nothing more…well, admiration. And that was dangerous to her.

"I need to change his diaper," she said, glad to have an excuse to bring this impromptu dinner to a close.

He yanked a thumb toward the door behind him. "I need to head out. I've stayed longer than I should have."

She wasn't about to suggest that he stick around—oh, no, that was not a good idea. She held Tate closer. "Okay, see you later. Sorry there was no meeting."

"You mean sorry we were set up?" He gave a light smile.

Was she sorry? Not exactly. "That's right. Watch out for the posse in the bushes."

He laughed as he strode toward the door. "I'll let myself out. You tend to that little guy."

She trailed him to the front door but held back a few feet. "See you."

"Yeah." He opened the door and grabbed his hat from the hat rack next to the door. Snugging it onto his head, holding her gaze the whole time. "Good night, Montana. You aren't half-bad."

She laughed. "You, either."

Grinning, he strode out, closing the door behind him. Through the bank of glass windows she watched him stride off toward his truck. His stride long and sure, his shoulders straight—she liked the proud, strong look of him. Especially after hearing about his childhood. "Not half-bad at all," she said to Tate. "Not half-bad at all."

Luke couldn't get the picture of Montana holding Tate in her arms out of his mind. Her bright eyes, her soft skin, and the gentle look of a loving mother touched him. He thought about that all the way home. She was focused, perceptive and interesting. He was drawn to that. As a rule, he didn't talk about his personal life on his dates. At least not like he and Montana had done. He didn't care to rehash a past that he hadn't enjoyed nor been able to control. He didn't like thinking about his dad. What kind of man would destroy his own life and then almost destroy his own sons? It was something he'd never understood. And nothing he'd ever talked about. Though there had been a moment there when

he'd been tempted to tell Montana everything. He'd been tempted to see what her
take on his dad would be. How she'd analyze
Leland Holden. She'd pegged his mom's mo-
tivations dead-on. Like hitting the nail with
a hammer in one strong strike she'd done so
with his mom. It was almost as if she understood because of insight. Deep insight that
only came from a true understanding.

Pulling into his carport, he turned off the
ignition and sat staring out at the darkness.
What in Montana Brown's background gave
her that kind of insight into his life?

Chapter Eleven

"Luke! Watch it—the calf," Jess yelled from where he was separating the calves from the herd. The air was thick with the sound and scent of dusty cattle.

"Sorry," Luke said. "My fault." He was supposed to be opening the gate.

"Where's your head, man? That's the fourth calf I've had to cut out again."

"It's on Montana," Colt called from where he was giving shots at the chute. "I heard he got set up last night."

"Oh, really now," Jess rested his arm on his saddle horn. "Why haven't I heard about this? I'm in town way more than Colt."

"I thought we were working cattle. Not talking about my private life."

That got hoots of laughter from both his brothers.

Colt gave the calf its shot, looking up as he released it from the steel chute. "Private. What's private about it? All they're talking about between conversations about the rodeo and festival is you and Montana. What I heard at the diner first thing this morning was the posse got you out there to a false committee meeting. App said you had dinner with Montana."

"How did App know?" Luke asked.

"He said Hank came in around six. Esther Mae had been out at Norma Sue's—at the real committee meeting—and came home all excited about you and Montana having dinner together."

Luke scowled. "How did they know we had dinner?"

"So you *did* have dinner." Jess was all ears now.

"I'm not denying it. I went out there thinking I was going to a committee meeting and it was just Montana watching Tate while Lacy and Clint went on a date. We ended up having dinner and talking."

"So, what did you think of her?" Colt stared at him through the bars of the squeeze chute. "I figured she might have sent you packing. Did she know it was a setup?"

"She realized what was going on before I did. And I like her. She's…" He paused, thinking about the evening. "She's observant and funny and interesting."

He saw the wide-eyed look that passed between his brothers. "What's wrong with that?"

Jess straightened in the saddle. "Nothin'. We didn't say anything. You, on the other hand, said plenty."

"I had dinner with her at her cousin's house with a sleeping baby. What's the big deal?" He wasn't sure why he was being so testy, but he was. He'd had dinner with other women, no big deal.

"Colt, you ever seen him get defensive over a woman?"

"Nope. Never. What's up with that, bro?"

"I'm defensive because we're supposed to be working."

"Not buying that." Jess shook his head. "You're the one letting the cows run free because your mind's on some cute cowgirl."

True, but Luke wasn't going to give them the satisfaction of an answer just so they could hound him endlessly. He could give as good as he got, though, and if roles were reversed, he'd more than likely be the one digging and teasing. He looked nonplussed. "Colt, don't you need to be done here and hit the road? I thought you had a string of bull-riding events lined up starting tonight?"

He grinned, pulled the lever and let the vaccinated calf free. "I've got time. Don't worry about me. I've got *plenty* of time to hear all about you and Montana."

Luke figured, sometimes it didn't pay to have brothers. There was just no pity there at all.

"Seriously, Luke, let's talk about this. You're thirty-four. We're out here working to build this business into something that we can pass on to our children. Something lasting. You know you aren't getting any younger."

Colt chuckled from behind the protection of the squeeze chute. "That's right, big brother. You might want to start thinking about starting that family, so you won't be too old to play with your children."

"Jess, you're thirty, that's not far behind me. And Colt, you're twenty-eight. One of you is going to have to step up before I do."

"You like this girl?" Jess asked, all kidding aside.

Luke could have shrugged it off, made a

joke, gone back to work. But his brothers understood him like no one else. It was a bond forged by years of taking care of each other. Teasing aside, he knew he could shoot straight with them. "Yeah, I do. There's something about her drive and determination that attracts me. I honestly haven't figured out what makes her different."

"That's easy," Colt called, as if Luke had just missed the obvious. "You like her because, unlike the ones who are looking to change you when they tell you they aren't—" Luke shot him a sharp look that had Colt throwing up his hands. "Hey, I'm telling it like I heard it. As I was saying—this gal thinks like you do."

Jess tapped his hand on his thigh. "Maybe you need to not think so much about how you aren't planning on getting serious, and let things just happen. Let yourself see where this leads."

"Yeah, what could it hurt?" Colt added.

"I know y'all mean well. But do I seem unhappy to y'all? What's the deal here?"

"Nothing," Jess said. "We just thought—"

Luke interrupted him. "I'm good, okay. Or I was, up until matchmakers started zeroing in on me, setting me up. And now y'all are ganging up on me. I'm fine, and whatever I do or don't do will be at my own time and pace."

Colt grinned, teasing, "Okay, okay, no need to get all in a huff. Right, Jess?"

"Yeah," Jess said, his own grin wide across his face. "Huffy isn't good on a cowboy such as yourself. Rest easy, we're not fixin' to tie you down and haul you to the altar."

"Jerks." Luke laughed, knowing they'd pushed his buttons and enjoyed watching him sweat bullets. "Get to work. We're burning daylight."

"What's the hurry? You got a date tonight?" Jess called, his chuckle moving wickedly over the breeze to blend with Colt's.

Luke hid his grin. *Brothers.*

The days after her "set-up dinner" with Luke flew by for Montana. She practiced her riding during the day, and helped out with Tate when she was needed. The baby spent some days with her and some with his mom and dad. The plans for the rodeo seemed to be falling in place and the excitement was building. Everywhere she went, they were talking about all the different people who'd been past residents of the tiny town who were coming back. The list included Adela's granddaughter Gabi. And Adela was very excited about that. Everyone knew that it was a long shot that any of the people would be able to actually move home. But like Norma Sue said, "Letting them come home to see the changes was a positive, and the attention they were drawing was always a good thing. Who knows, maybe some would find a way. And maybe some would fall in love."

Of course, she'd been looking right at Montana when she made that last statement. Montana'd been getting a lot of that over the last two weeks.

Ever since Luke had shown up at her house, it had been on lots of minds. She wasn't saying much, just shrugging it off with a snappy retort, finding that teasing about it was about as easy a way out as anything. And besides, she and Luke had an understanding. They both knew they weren't looking for love, and that was all that mattered.

The fact that she now found the cowboy very likable and extremely attractive was no big deal—really. It was as if knowing they were on the same page helped her relax around him. Not that they were going on any more dates, but when she saw him she was able to not be on the defensive.

There was, however, the problem of Erica. The woman had issues. Montana had run into her a couple of times, and both times had been awkward, since Erica had ignored her when Montana had spoken. One of those times had been at church—which seemed a very odd place for someone to act that way. What Montana wanted to know was what she had done to the woman. Montana noticed that she had behaved the same way to Luke when he'd given her a casual hello. If only Erica would just move on. However, Montana didn't let it bother her.

She wasn't in the wrong. Luke and Erica were not an item and never had been. He'd made it clear from the beginning that he wasn't in the market. But Erica had ignored his warning. She was out of line—she needed to accept responsibility for her mistake and move on.

Speaking of out of line, Montana was straightening up a barrel that was way off base from where it should be. One of the cowboys who worked for Clint had driven the tractor around, spreading and refreshing the dirt during lunch. He hadn't been exactly worried about where he placed her three barrels when he was done. They were way out of line—but if she could handle Erica's bad attitude, she could handle fixing a few barrels.

"Hey, cowgirl, they making you move your own barrels around these days?"

At the sound of Luke's voice, she spun around to find him watching her from the other side of the pen. Her heart did the wacky little jangle it had started doing when he was around; she promptly ignored it. Giving him a cocky grin, she walked toward where he was standing. "Yup, I can't prove it, but I think Clint's trying to get me in better shape for the event, so he told Bill to move them way out of line, so I'd have to wrestle 'em into place. It's a workout but it's all good." She flexed her muscle. "These babies are growing by the day."

He squinted at her arm. "You sure you call that a muscle?"

The beeper he wore on his belt suddenly went off. He snatched it up and stared at the message. "Fire at Esther Mae Wilcox's place," he said, his words clipped. "I'm on the volunteer fire department. I've got to go."

"But wait," she called, already having

climbed to the top of the fence and thrown a leg over. She was about to jump to the ground when he turned, reached up and lifted her down.

"Sorry, gotta go," he said, then headed at a trot toward the exit.

Obviously, the cowboy had misunderstood, thinking her call to wait was a call for help off the fence. She jogged after him, her mind on Esther Mae's fire. She hoped it wasn't bad. "I'm going with you," she said, rounding the truck as he was yanking open his driver's side door.

He had the truck cranked by the time she had her door opened and had slung herself into the seat beside him.

"You sure?" he asked, already backing out to turn the truck in the right direction.

"Sure I'm sure. You might need help, so hit the gas, buddy!"

He nodded and punched the gas. They peeled out of the drive, and from across the pasture she could see Clint's black truck spraying gravel as he tore up one of the roads snaking deeper into the ranch. Clint and several of his ranch hands were on the volunteer fire department, too.

The sun beamed down hot as they sped

past the area designated for the festival. Starting tomorrow, which was Wednesday, the vendors would start turning up, and by Friday the festivities would begin. But none of that mattered as she thought of Esther Mae and Hank. And the fire. She prayed they were all right. Prayed for their safety.

Luke snatched up a radio handset and shot questions at the dispatcher. It was a grease fire. Esther Mae had called it in. Hank was home, but out in the pasture somewhere. She was trying to put it out herself.

"That's not good," Luke said, his expression growing grimmer. "Esther Mae is so excitable, she might get burned if she tries to deal with burning grease."

"The house isn't worth her getting hurt." Montana started praying harder for God to protect Esther Mae, and that the fire would be easily contained.

The radio crackled, alive with communication, as men all across the community reacted. "You don't have to go to town for your gear?" she asked when she realized they weren't heading toward town.

"It's in my tack box in the truck bed. Clint will go to town and get the truck."

"There isn't any smoke," Montana observed

a few minutes later as the house came into view. "Oh, look there they are! On the front porch." Relief swamped her.

"They look okay. That's a blessing."

"Oh, my gracious!" Esther Mae exclaimed, flying off the porch to greet them with excited hugs. "Y'all got here so fast! Thank the good Lord."

Her yellow shirt was smeared with something white, and her flaming red hair and face looked like they had been rained on with flour. Her long, yellow shorts were streaked and the bottoms of them were dripping wet. Her right side was splotchy with water, too. Hank sat on the porch looking glum, totally drenched from head to toe. He held an ice pack to his forehead, and beneath it was a large purple knot.

"What happened to you?" Montana and Luke almost said in unison. Other trucks were pulling in behind them, and there was small crowd of firefighting cowboys gathering, asking questions, too. Hank frowned and didn't look at all enthused to speak.

"Oh, Hank came to my rescue…" Esther Mae gushed, ever so happy to share. "At least he tried. See, I was frying up some catfish for lunch. And Norma Sue called on the phone—" She paused, shooting Luke and Montana a pink-tinged glance. "We were, um, talking—and I walked into the other room for a few minutes and forgot about the grease. When I came back in, it had started flaming. I screamed and called 911—I still had the phone in my hand. Then I ran to the door and shouted, 'Fire!' Hank was working in the barn and I was sure hoping he could hear me."

Hank rolled his eyes and shook his head, looking more and more like he had a bigger headache coming on than the goose egg growing on his forehead.

"Did you get that bump when you were putting the fire out?" Montana asked.

Hank grunted, turned a deep shade of magenta. "Not exactly."

"See, I shouted for Hank to bring water. I meant the water hose, but I guess the first thing that hit him was the cow pond. He grabbed up a bucket and bolted toward that pond as fast as a man his age can go. I don't know what I was more shocked at, him running or the fire! Well, I turned back to the kitchen and the flames were shooting up toward the ceiling, I gasped and let go of the door, and you aren't going to believe this, but the wind suddenly came up out of no-where, slammed that door back, ramming it up against the wall so hard that it shook the shelves on the wall above the fire flaming on the stove. The giant can of baking soda sitting up there fell off the shelf, knocking the lid off, and showered down on the fire and me like rain from the good Lord! It was a plum beautiful sight—and a miracle for certain." Esther Mae blinked back tears and beamed happily at them all.

Everyone was silent, glad the fire was out, amazed how it had happened, but still puzzled. What about Hank?

It was suddenly apparent that whatever had happened to Hank must have been embarrassing, and no one was asking questions. Montana had to know, though.

"So, what about Hank?" she asked. Everyone leaned in a little closer.

Esther Mae's head tilted. "I hurried to holler at Hank that it was okay. He'd just reached the pier and was breathing hard, but when I yelled he looked at me and he tripped."

"Yep, I tripped."

Esther Mae placed her hand on his shoulder and looked down at him. "Tripped on the edge of the water, and it's shallow and muddy there. He skidded across that muddy water and slammed his head right into the pier. I had to run down there and fish him out."

Hank raised his head up, ice pack and all, and met Montana's eyes first. And the most amazing thing happened…his lip twitched at the edge. His eyes twinkled, like the first glow of a star at night. When his lip twitched more, so did Montana's. And then Hank chuckled.

Montana chuckled with him, and then like popcorn beginning to pop, chuckles erupted one by one through the group.

"Oh, Hank," Esther Mae cooed, plopping down beside him and hugging him. "That's my man. And you really did stop the fire. You're the one who put that monster can of baking soda up there, just in case there ever was a fire."

Hank patted his wife's hand and beamed when she leaned in and gave him a kiss on the cheek. And suddenly all in the world was right.

Chapter Twelve

"That was the sweetest thing I've ever seen," Montana said. She and Luke were driving back toward the ranch. "Hank was so embarrassed, but then it hit him that it could have been so much worse."

"Esther Mae cracks me up," Luke added. "I didn't think she was ever going to get the story told. And there sat poor Hank, dripping wet, with the lump on his forehead growing by the second."

Montana laughed at Luke's humor. "Here I thought you were feeling sympathetic toward Hank's situation."

"I was. Poor guy. I knew something was up when he wasn't saying anything. But I couldn't figure out how he got so wet."

"I'm just glad they were all right. And their house looked pretty good, considering what it could have been. I'm sure it will smell like burned grease for a few days, but for there not to be much flame damage shocked me."

"They were lucky. And what little damage that was done, Cole Turner can have changed out in a day. Fixing disasters is what he does."

She sighed, feeling good. "I'm really glad it turned out like that."

He glanced at her and slowed at a dirt road that split off the main road. "Thanks for coming along. You were great in there, helping clean up like you did."

"I didn't do much. Not after Norma Sue and Adela arrived."

"You got it started until you got booted out."

Montana hooted. "Ha. It was so obvious that they wanted us to leave and go get this trailer full of calves you said you needed to move."

"Are you sure you're okay with this?"

"I guess so. I know this is just your way of trying to get another date, but really, Luke, getting Esther Mae to almost burn her house down is taking it a bit too far."

"Yeah, that's even too extreme for the matchmakers."

"True, but how about you?"

His eyes twinkled when he looked at her. "I'm thinking right now that it's all working out real fine."

Montana felt a warm glow fill her at his words and the look in his eyes. She hadn't expected flattery. "You surprise me," she said quietly.

"Yeah? How's that?"

"You're sweet. I mean, I thought Hank and Esther Mae were sweet but I wasn't expecting you to be sweet."

"And you say that with such conviction."

She laughed at his dry tone. "Thanks, I really try hard," she said drily, mocking his tone and making them both smile at the teasing banter between them.

His ranch was neat, the wood fence around the small ranch house was old but had a fresh coat of black on it and the house looked as if it had just been painted, too. The white exterior gleamed in the clear May sunshine, making the black shutters and front door stand out. She liked the way it looked. The barn was a faded red that had withstood many years, but looked sturdy and very neat. She could tell just looking around that Luke and his brothers hadn't bought the newest place in town, but it had good bones, and the land surrounding it was flat and full of cattle. Like most places it looked like the lack of rain was affecting it. But it was still pretty land.

"I like your place."

He surveyed the land through the truck's windows. "Thanks. We're proud of it." They drove past the house and down the lane to a stockyard where a trailer was backed up to the loading pen. They got out and he opened the gate. A truck whipped in as they were getting out and a man hopped from it.

"You must be the one and only Montana Brown." Striding up and holding out his hand, he grinned. "I'm Jess, Luke's brother."

"Hi, Jess. I'm almost afraid to ask what you've heard about me."

He gave a cocky grin, his amber eyes lit with humor. "Oh, it's all good, I guess, if you don't mind being the talk of the town and all."

"The matchmakers?"

He chuckled. "And App and Stanley. And Sam. Stanley was singing your praises again this morning when I went in for coffee and eggs. Seems you've made a friend for life, rescuing him with warm soup and your big, bright smile."

Montana felt warm inside, knowing she'd done the right thing taking that soup to him. "Luke helped, too."

Jess gave his brother an appraising glance. "He drove, no big deal. It's the smile and warm heart of a pretty woman that Stanley remembers. That's what helped him heal up 'lickety-split,' as he put it this morning."

"I didn't do anything but be the delivery girl."

"So be it, but you'll have a fan rootin' for you loud and long come Friday night when you're out there blasting around those barrels."

"After the fire today, she'll have a couple of others doing the same where Esther Mae and Hank Wilcox are concerned."

"Fire? What fire? Did I miss something?"

Luke filled him in on what had just transpired out at Esther Mae's. When he was done, Jess flashed his pearly whites at her again. She had a feeling he was a heartbreaker like his brother. Like his brother, she wondered if he walked around grinning and smiling and leaving a trail of women behind with broken hearts and dashed dreams of happily-ever-after.

"Y'all keep it up and you'll both be up for

the Mule Hollow Good Samaritan Award." Jess gave them a thumbs-up.

Luke grunted and turned to the pen full of calves. "I'm fixin' ta move 'em in if you'll work this end."

"Sure thing." Jess winked at her and then went to man the gate.

Luke was taking the teasing fairly good-naturedly. She wondered, when she wasn't around, if it was better or worse. "I'll help," she said, and followed Luke into the pen.

"You don't need—"

"Hey, I came to help, remember? And I do know a little about livestock."

"As you wish. Just stay clear of them. I don't want you getting slammed up against the rails or anything."

"You got it, pardner."

They made quick work of herding the load onto the trailer, and then left the grinning Jess standing in the drive as they took off once more.

"You must get teased all the time." Her observation drew one of his nonchalant shrugs.

"It comes with baby brothers."

"Is your other brother as bad?" she asked.

"He has his moments. He's a bull rider

and stays out on the road more than Jess. We don't see him as often as we like, but he's going after his dreams. He's down in Mesquite this week, riding in a PBR event. Then he'll be here late Friday night, in time to catch the bull event here in town before heading to another event on Saturday night. Like you, he has a shot at the big time if he holds out and doesn't make a mistake."

She scowled at him. "You saying I'm going to make a mistake?"

He wasn't smiling when he looked at her. "Nope. I'm saying you're good, Montana. Real good. And if you keep putting in the time and start hauling to rodeos and making the points…" He paused, gave a small, serious little smile that evoked a feeling of encouragement that shot straight to her heart. "You do that, and you know as well as I do that you can go all the way to the finals and take it."

Montana's heart clutched in her chest, looking at the sincerity in his eyes and hearing it in his words. It was her cowgirl dream, and suddenly she felt energized and lifted up.

A lump lodged in her throat. When she managed to get past it, she grinned and teased him. "You're just sayin' that because you're still trying to get a date with me?"

"That'd be an affirmative on the still-trying-to-get-a-date front. And you did just say I was sweet." He batted his chocolate eyes at her, and her insides quivered like gelatin.

"Funny man." Pretending this wasn't getting to her was hard work!

"Hey, gotta try. And what I said is the truth, too. God gives us all talent in different areas. I don't know you well enough to know what all kinds of talents He gave you, but I've known from day one of seeing you ride that when it comes to barrel racing, you've got it. He loaded you up with that talent, and with drive and heart, too. It's an unbeatable combination. You don't need to waste it."

There was a lot the handsome cowboy could have said. A lot she would have expected only a few weeks earlier from her first impressions of him. This wasn't any of it.

This touched her deeper than he could know. "Thank you," she said, unable to find the right words. His smile warmed her heart. Suddenly feeling like the inside of the truck was too small, she studied the countryside as they rode. They were quiet the rest of the way back to the ranch. When he pulled up to the barn, she was relieved. She needed some space. She might have been quiet on the ride, but her thoughts had been full of Luke and what he'd said. *He believed in her*.

She found that extremely appealing.

That she could handle, but it wasn't that she was thinking about. Nope. She was thinking about a kiss.

She'd been curious about his past, curious about his thoughts and what made the cowboy tick. And now he'd gone and had her wondering what it would be like to be held in the arms of a man who believed in her. Mostly, she wondered what it would feel like to have his lips meet hers.

Yep, her feet had just lost touch with the bottom of the pond and she was dog-paddling in murky waters. She wasn't supposed to be wanting to kiss anybody! She wasn't supposed to be thinking about falling in love!

But sometimes a gal couldn't control her thoughts, especially when a man said all the right things—meant them.

That was exactly why, the minute they got to the ranch, she made her excuses and headed back to the house with a closed door between them.

She needed time to get her head on straight.

* * *

On Thursday, the ranch was buzzing with activity. Lacy had taken off work for the next three days and it was a good thing. It was chaos. Vendors were pulling into the ranch lane with their snow cone trailers, dog-on-a-stick shacks, kettle-corn setups and so much more. Montana was able to hole up in the arena and practice during the morning, but it was impossible soon after that. Livestock was arriving by the trailer loads, too. And the bulls! Hulking bulls that looked as mean as the reputations that preceded them, began being delivered from various sources.

Luke was in and out, moving animals and helping make certain all manner of things were taken care of for the rodeo. Montana had been thinking about him more than was good, and tried to avoid him as much as possible. Since there was so much going on with the rodeo, avoiding him wasn't all that difficult.

She was with Lacy when Lilly and Cort Wells came into the barn. They were in charge of the petting zoo on both Friday and Saturday, but also helped with the rodeos at night. Samantha, their mischief-making donkey, was always the star attraction at the zoo, and she was going to be housed in a stall in the barn on Friday night.

They were a great couple, and were in the process of adopting a set of twins. Montana laughed when they told her how they met and how Samantha had had a part in their matchmaking. From what they said, she was an escape artist that liked to roam instead of stay in her stall. Because of this, Lilly was a little worried about her getting loose and interrupting the rodeo, so they'd come to look at her stall to see what precautions needed to be made to ensure she didn't escape.

Montana went with them to check things out, and had to agree that it would need a little something to hold it shut better. All a smart animal would have to do was nudge the latch up with its nose and be free. Not a good thing.

The matchmaking posse drove up just as they were exiting the barn. Cort went to find Clint. Lilly, Lacy and Montana went to help the posse set up the concession stand.

"Hold your horses," Norma Sue said when Esther Mae started toward the grill. "You are not getting near the grill."

"I'm not, but I wouldn't have caught anything on fire if you hadn't called me," Esther

Mae shot back with a chuckle, looking happy. "I tell you girls, there is nothing like a near miss to make a body realize how blessed they are. I very nearly lost my house. Of course, a house is just a house, and my Hank banged his head on the pier and nearly drowned. If I hadn't been there—now that would have been a loss I couldn't have stood. I'm a very blessed woman."

As she was speaking, everyone had jumped in and started organizing different areas. Lacy was putting cups up on a shelf and paused.

"I know what you mean, Esther Mae. When I finally got pregnant with Tate, I was just so overjoyed. I really, really was. I mean, I'd finally come to grips with the fact that God might have a different plan for me and Clint. Like he did with you and Cort, Lilly. But then, when I conceived…I felt so very blessed. It's amazing the way we can take things for granted, isn't it?"

"It really is," Lilly joined in. "Me and Cort understood, even before we were married, that he couldn't have children. We felt blessed that we had Joshua." She smiled, showing off her dimples. "My grannies might not have ever had any luck with men, but I tell you, I got such a treasure in Cort. He might not be Joshua's biological daddy but he *is* his daddy. And he is going to be the most wonderful daddy to our new boys."

"Yes, he is," Adela said, opening napkins and placing them in a holder. "Psalms 107:21 tells us to give thanks to the Lord for his unfailing love and his wonderful deeds for men." She smiled sweetly. "I love when I hear young people like you two giving Him the glory He so deserves. He likes it, too."

Montana was filling the ice chest with sodas and was glad she was off to the side, away from everyone. Her thoughts were filled suddenly with how disgruntled she'd been feeling about her parents' divorce and the way her life had been before coming here to Mule Hollow. She didn't look up as she took soda after soda and placed it in the insulated container. She felt so deeply ashamed. In thinking about the things in her life that she was *dis*satisfied with, had she lost sight of the blessings God had bestowed on her? The thought settled on her like a mudslide.

Chapter Thirteen

"This has been a long one," Jess said at the end of the day. "See you in the morning, bro," he called, looking at Luke out the open window of his truck.

"I'm not far behind you," Luke said. "It's going to be a long day tomorrow, too." After watching Jess leave, he headed toward his truck but found himself detouring into the barn, heading toward Murdock's stall. Montana had disappeared in that direction earlier. With the festival there on the premises, it was a fairly congested area, and he'd been lucky to see her at all.

He found her in the far corner, sitting alone on a five-gallon bucket. "What's up? You look like you lost your best friend. Are you worn out?"

She looked up at him with serious eyes,

more blue than green in the shadows. "Have you ever realized you were a jerk?"

This didn't sound good. "What did I do now?"

Her eyes widened and she huffed a short laugh. "No, not *you. I'm* the jerk."

Her gaze shifted from him to some far-off place in her thoughts. He spied another feed bucket, snagged it up, flipped it over and sat down in her line of vision. "You aren't a jerk. Talk to me."

"I was listening to everyone working in the concession stand talk about all their blessings. Everyone was looking at all the good things God's done in their lives. Despite the fact that there were lots of bad things happening. It made me think about where my head has been since I came here. I honestly can't remember the last time I actually thanked God for all the good things He's done for me. And He has given me tons of things to be thankful for—like coming here, for instance. It's been wonderful to have Lacy and Clint's home to come to, and to have a place to ride Murdock. It's been great to spend time with Tate, Lacy and Clint."

"And me?" he teased.

"Yes, it's been a real blessing getting to know you. And that's a big shock to me."

He dipped his brows into a mocking scowl. "Hey, you were on a roll till that."

She gave a light huff, and seemed to relax doing so. "I'm just being honest. I did think you were a bit of a jerk when I first met you. But then I changed my mind."

"I'm glad about that. And even if you hadn't changed it, you still aren't a jerk. Lots of people lose sight of the good things in their lives when they've got junk from their past filling up their days. It's not always easy to let things go. Believe me, I know that from experience." He felt as if something about her parents' divorce was bothering her, but he wouldn't ask. She'd tell him if she wanted. He wasn't sure how exactly she viewed him. Sure, they'd become friends in a way. It was a little hard to explain *what* they'd become. He knew that he enjoyed being around her, his world did tricks when he was around her…he was more relaxed when he was near her, but at the same time he was tense. He couldn't concentrate when she was around because he kept getting distracted lately with the idea of kissing her. If he kissed her, she'd probably slap him and call him a jerk for sure. Which wouldn't be a good thing. Wait! What was he doing? Here he was sitting here, trying to figure out what was wrong with Montana and suddenly he was thinking about kissing?

Yup, not good.

"I'm not sure what's bothering you, but if I can help, I'm here." She could choose to talk or not. He realized he wished she would feel comfortable enough to talk to him. He wanted to get closer to her. The idea startled him a bit. It was different than when he'd dated other women. Different than just feeling attracted to a woman. He was trying to wrap his emotions around it and understand.

"I've come here to try and fulfill my dream of being a cowgirl. That's what I'm doing. But I gave it up years ago to become the career woman that my dad wanted me to be. You're supposed to do what your parents want—right?"

Not exactly. He thought of his dad. If he'd done what his dad had wanted, he'd be wallowing in self-pity, spending his days looking for the next bottle.

But that was not what Montana needed to hear. "To an extent," he said, quietly finding his way. The anger that he'd sensed in her from day one had crept back into her voice. Her attitude was locked up with it.

"I knew what I wanted to do with my life. I could have been a champion. I may still be able to be one—but I've been filled with a lot of resentment lately, and it's overshadowed everything in my life these last few months. I turned everything upside down on a whim, and came out here to stay with Lacy."

"My first question is, why all of a sudden are you having these feelings? Didn't you resent it all when you gave up your dream?"

"My dad." Her words were full of anger. She took a breath, visibly calming herself as she started over. "My dad pushed me to be what he felt was of greater status. He was very aware of how and what others thought of us as a family. He thought riding was a great thing for me to do during my school years, but that should stop there. I was expected to go to college and get the accounting degree he felt would be appropriate. *Pro rodeo cowgirl* just didn't have the right ring to it."

Montana had been the good girl and done as her dad wanted. "But why are you suddenly rebelling and doing what you want? Why all the resentment now? The divorce?"

She stood and walked a few paces away

before she turned, and he saw the flash of fire in her eyes. "Partly. But mostly because of his affair. When I found out about that, I hit the road."

"You can't let this eat you up. Believe me, I know."

He went to her, wanting to brush the strands of hair from her face that had escaped her braid. "I can remember the first time I understood that my dad had a drinking problem. Like I told you before, I was young. I don't even remember how old I was, but I remember the fights my parents had. There was nothing physical, only bitter blowouts. This particular day, my mom was crying in the bathroom and I asked my dad why he always made my momma cry. He told me she'd known he drank when she married him, and so she had no reason to always be harping on him. And then I watched him lift the bottle up and drink the whole thing without stopping. It made me sick watching. He looked at me and told me for the first time— of many—that I would be just like him." He paused, remembering. It still made him sick thinking about it. "I never will forget that. I was young but I knew then that I didn't want to be like him. I wasn't sure if what he said was a fact—being young I didn't understand exactly. I just knew I didn't want it. I grew up quick after that."

"I'm so sorry." She laid her hand on his arm and the warmth seeped into his skin.

"It happened a very long time ago. And like I told you the other night, God helped me move on."

"Still, you don't get angry?"

"Yeah, actually, I did. I didn't have the feeling of betrayal that's shadowing you, but I resented that he was my dad. Unlike you, there were no expectations for me. You're resentful because you were pinned to your dad's hopes and dreams because you were doing what you knew was right." He could tell that hit a mark. "You were honoring God's plan by honoring your dad, doing what he expected of you."

"And he let me down."

"Yes, he did. My dad let me down, too, but it was out in the open. No surprises. That was just the way it was. Whereas you were blindsided by it. And now, the way I see it, you're still staggering from being thrown off the bull and mowed down. You're entitled to some resentment."

She stiffened, pulling her shoulders back. "I've got that. No doubt about it."

"Look. We don't get to pick our parents. But we get to pick who we'll become. That's what I'm doing. I don't know if you know about Clint's mom, but in a way, she did what your dad did. She left, and it was real hard on Clint and his dad. But Mac remained hardworking, honest and someone I could look up to. I started working for him the day we moved to town when I was fifteen. He was a great influence in my life."

"I've heard Clint talk about his dad. He built this ranch on hard work and honesty. Clint has carried that out and expanded every aspect. Lacy is so proud of him and the man that he is."

She sighed, looking lost. "I used to be proud of my dad. I believed he was an honorable man. I believed he loved my mother. I've been torn up over this—mad, furious, and torn by the idea that I'm somehow supposed to forgive him for making me feel this way. *Enough* of this." She waved her hand, as if shooing the thoughts away. "Anyway— it hit me today that this stuff is all I've been focusing on. It's horrible how I've forgotten what good things God has done for me. I'm going to try to be more positive."

He put his hands on her shoulders. Couldn't help it. "Good. That's what you need to do for now. You can deal with these feelings later, but you need to clear your head tonight and get ready for tomorrow. You need to put this all out of your head and get in the zone. Murdock is counting on you." He grinned, knowing she wanted to make her horse proud. "You've got this in the bag if you just get your focus on the ride tomorrow night. Maybe it's nerves shaking you up right now."

"Maybe. Some of it."

"Focus, Montana Brown—cowgirl extraordinaire." That got a tiny smile from her and he touched his forehead against hers. When she didn't draw away, that got a big smile from him. "Ride like the wind tomorrow night and make yourself proud." Pulling back, he looked sternly into her eyes. "Don't ride with anger. Don't ride to prove anything to anyone but yourself. And God. He's the one who gave you this talent, and you've been working hard to polish it up. That's all you can do, is give it your all. This other stuff…it'll work itself out in time."

She leaned her head on his chest and nodded. He pulled her into his arms and hugged her. Just held her close, giving her the comfort and support that he knew she needed. He liked being able to be there for her in this moment. Again, she drew him, just as she'd been doing from the first day he saw her.

And he wasn't exactly sure what to do about it.

Chapter Fourteen

It was a gorgeous, sunny day for the festival.

"Isn't that just the cutest thing," Esther Mae cooed, waving at Tate. He was dressed in a baby cowboy outfit, complete with chaps and was sitting on the top of the fattest little donkey Montana had ever seen.

Samantha the donkey was adorable. She was gray with white whiskers, and so fat that she had rolls rippling from her shoulders to her hips. She had big, brown, mischievous eyes, and when she batted her eyelashes it made Montana wonder what the little gal was thinking about. Tate was loving his time spent being held on her back. There was no doubt that, with all the cowboys in his life, Tate would be a cowboy himself someday.

"He loves it," Lacy said, beaming at him as she held him. He stuffed his fist in his mouth, grinning at his mom, then everyone else, when they oohed at him. He was enjoying being the center of attention. At six months old, he was already a big flirt with his big blue eyes.

"Yoo-hoo, Luke," Esther Mae hollered suddenly, startling everyone including Samantha, who popped her head up, looking past Montana to see what the fuss was. Everyone, including Montana, turned to see Luke striding toward them.

"I thought you were fixin' to walk past us," Esther Mae said, looking more mischievous than Samantha ever thought about.

Luke's gaze met Montana's and she saw his own glint of mischief. "I thought about it, Esther Mae, but with all you pretty women standing over here, I wouldn't have been able to pass y'all by."

Montana almost laughed at the twinkle in Luke's eyes. The instant she'd heard Esther Mae yell his name, her pulse had jumped into overdrive. He'd been so supportive last night, and she was still mesmerized by how safe and comforted she'd felt, wrapped in his arms. She'd had a hard time pulling back and watching him leave. Her heart had sighed as he'd driven away, leaving her standing on the front porch. She was glad the house was silent as she'd entered because she was sure Lacy would have seen her float up the stairs.

Montana Brown, cowgirl wannabe, was in danger of falling in love.

"What are you doing right now?" Norma Sue asked, walking over to stand near him. Hooking her thumbs in the straps of her overalls, she studied him intently. "You don't look like you got much sleep last night."

Montana looked closer at him, and didn't see what Norma Sue was talking about. The man looked absolutely perfect. His coffee-colored eyes looked bright and alert to her. They widened at the ranch woman's comment.

"I slept like a baby."

"Good!" Esther Mae exclaimed. "Then you can take this one—" she shocked Montana by placing her hands on Montana's back and pushing her toward him "—over to the competitions and join in. I hear they're going to have a three-legged race any minute, and that's always a good one to—"

Adela stepped up and broke Esther Mae off. "It's a good one to get the heart pumping and the laughter flowing."

Esther Mae crossed her arms over her peacock-blue blouse and harrumphed. "It's also good to get to know your partner. And don't forget about the octopus ride!"

"I wasn't planning on joining in any games," Montana said.

Lacy chuckled, looking at Tate. She rubbed noses with him, and he grabbed at her hair. "Oh, no, you don't. Hey." She continued looking at Montana. "I'm going to go feed him and then I'm coming back to defend my championship title in the cow chip throwing competition. I'm officially challenging you. Every cowgirl needs to know how to toss one of those bad boys."

"I wasn't—" Montana was feeling a bit trapped. The light in Luke's eyes told her he knew how she felt, but he was also very amused by the situation. He had no clue how trapped she was feeling, how seriously her feelings were changing where he was concerned. She'd known it the moment she opened her eyes that morning. Looking at Lacy, she couldn't say no. "Okay," she agreed. "I'll be there, and you better come prepared. Because, believe it or not, I can toss a chip a very long way."

And so, she found herself walking through the crowd beside Luke, and feeling as if she was heading down a wrong-way street with her hands tied behind her back. Luke, on the other hand, looked like he was on the same road but totally enjoying the crazy ride, judging by the twitch of his lips when he looked at her.

"So you actually throw cow patties?"

"Haven't done it in a while—probably a decade—but I can."

As they wove through the crowd, he gave her a disbelieving glance. "You touched them?"

"That'd be a *nooo*. I wore gloves. Those things are—well, you know what they are. I'm not touching it. But I can sure give my cousin a run for the money."

"I have no doubt about that. How about tonight? Are you ready for the barrel racing?"

"Yes, I am. But I think the three-legged race is going to be a great warm-up for me. The posse was right. This is a good thing, you and me."

"Stuck like glue," he said.

Montana chuckled. "That's right. You and me, babe."

Luke laughed. The low, husky sound made Montana's pulse dance.

They walked past booth after booth of

handmade crafts, tons of jewelry and half a dozen food trailers. Luke stopped in front of a burger booth. "I've got to eat something before we race."

"That's good thinking. I wouldn't want to lose because you were slacking."

"Oh, you don't have to worry about that. I can handle myself."

She put her hands on her hips and made herself not laugh. "A little competitive, are we?"

He tapped her nose with his index finger. "And don't you forget it."

"Then we're a great match." The words were out of her mouth before she realized what she was saying. Looking at him, his eyes twinkling, she decided maybe now would be a good time to stop speaking. The look in his eyes told her he might be wondering the same thing. Suddenly she was wondering, *were* they a great match? She flashed back to being in his arms, and it struck her like lightning that they were.

She took a step back. Her arm had been lightly touching his, standing in line. Suddenly, feeling a little faint, she wanted to sit down or pass out. She didn't have time to be getting crazy. She didn't have time to be thinking things she hadn't been thinking in a very long time.

She didn't trust men. Right?

She didn't want a man in her life. Right?

She didn't want to fall in love. Right?

But he was great. He was unbelievably sincere. He was funny. He was…easy to fall in love with.

Oh, my goodness—she was in trouble.

His eyebrows crinkled as he looked at her strangely. "Are you okay?"

She slapped a hand to her stomach. "Nerves," she squeaked, gasping a little.

"Really? You're white. Come on." Taking her arm, he led her out of the line and toward a spot behind all the booths, away from the traffic. They'd used square bales of hay in some areas to give seating to weary festival goers, and Luke spotted a pile of extra hay. Leading her to it immediately, he gently pushed her down to sit.

"I'm fine," she said. "Really I am." She was seeing black spots.

He knelt down in front of her and his concerned brown eyes seemed to melt into her as he searched hers. He touched her forehead with his fingers. She gasped at his touch and then stuck her head between her knees and gasped for air.

"Breathe, Montana, breathe." Luke rubbed Montana's back. He wasn't sure what was going on. One minute she'd been fine—teasing and rattling on and making him laugh. Then all of a sudden, she'd turned as white as a sheet and was threatening to pass out.

"I'm fine," she groaned after a minute, and sat up, looking more stunned than anything.

She was staring at him like he had two heads. "Did I do something wrong? Are you sure this is about your ride tonight?" He'd been thinking about her all night long. He'd never had a woman on his mind like he had Montana. He'd done his best to steer clear of her all morning because he wanted to see her so bad. Maybe she'd wanted him to show up this morning. Maybe she was mad at him. Maybe that was a good thing—he wasn't certain.

"No, you didn't do anything wrong."

He leaned forward. She sucked in a breath and leaned back, keeping him at a distance. "Okay, then what's up?"

She shook her head as if trying to clear it, and then shot up from the hay, glaring at him. "I don't want this."

"Want what?" he asked, maintaining his calm in the midst of a growing gale.

"This." She waved a hand toward him, then back toward herself. "This, this *thing* that's happening between us. And don't try and deny it, because I know you feel it, too. Or maybe you don't."

He shouldn't think she was cute. But he did. That made him smile inside. He honestly liked everything about Montana Brown, including her odd tendency to get mad at herself when she was feeling things she didn't like...or felt threatened by. He grinned at her, despite the fact that it was thoughts of him that were making her so mad.

"I do know I enjoy being around you. But right now, I'm also looking forward to you and me smoking a bunch of three-legged couples in a few minutes. You know what I think?" He scratched his jaw, then crossed his arms and studied her.

"What?" She glared at him but paused her pacing.

"I think you need to relax. You're making more out of this than it is." He needed her to calm down. "The fact is that I like you and you like me. No big deal. We're still in control of what we do with that. Right?" He nodded, slowly urging her to agree.

She looked a bit puzzled, but nodded in response to his. "Yes."

"Good, then relax and let's go win a race. And don't forget, I want to see you chuck a cow chip farther than anyone else."

Chapter Fifteen

"You ready for this?" Luke asked Montana as they tugged the feed sack over their legs. They'd tied her left leg to his right leg with the twine that Stanley handed them.

"I'm always ready for a little competition," she said, narrowing her eyes, teasingly preparing for battle. She let her gaze swing slowly around the gathering group, sizing up the competitors.

"You're looking serious. I need to warn you that I've never done this before, so I hope you don't get too disappointed."

"Hey, you need to focus, Luke Holden. Focus and get a little can-do spirit. Look at me." She took his face between her hands and turned his face toward her. "Now read my lips and repeat after me. 'I can do this.'"

He chuckled. "I can do this."

"See, it's all better now. We're going to do this, aren't we, fellas?"

Stanley and App were standing in front of them. Each man had his arms crossed over his chest as he studied them with critical eyes.

"You might better tighten up that thar string," App grunted.

"That's right. Too much slack can lead to tripping," Stanley said, looking like he wanted to jump in and take over the tying.

Luke grinned as he reached down and studied the string once more. "I've got it handled, Stanley. Don't worry." He shook the string, noting that it was loose but comfortable.

"I don't know about that. It still looks a little loose. A loose string kin trip you up and throw off yor hop-'n'-run move."

"Hop-'n'-run move? What's that?" Montana asked, getting a kick out of Stanley's serious attitude.

"It's the way you get the job done," he said.

"Yup," App butted in. "You hop together— like this. Then you run one step together with the outside legs—like this."

Everyone around enjoyed the demonstration from Applegate. The skinny stick of a man was dressed in his starched jeans and shirt, topped off with his pristine, go-to-town straw Stetson—he'd explained to her the difference earlier, when she'd told him she liked his new hat. He'd beamed and told her it wasn't new, it was just the one he wore to church on Sunday. His everyday hat had gotten eaten by an ornery old goat at the petting zoo. "I had to go home and get my church hat—stinking goat. I couldn't be up here at the rodeo without wearing a hat." Montana smiled as she watched his demonstration carefully.

"We can do that," she said to Luke.

He nodded seriously, and showed her some of his new can-do spirit. "Sure we can. Would you mind doing that again, App? Just in case we didn't get it the first time."

App frowned. "It ain't that easy ta do. Yor tryin' ta be funny, Luke Holden, but I'm tellin' ya, this is the move ta win…." His voice trailed off when Erica walked up with a cowboy in tow. She glared at Montana and then at Luke, before she snatched the string and burlap sack from Stanley, who'd shut his mouth the instant he saw her walk up and held out the armload of bags he had to hand out.

She sat on the hay bale across from Montana and gave her the evil eye. Montana thought it was a little ridiculous that she was continuing to act the way she was. Montana looked away, while Luke was concentrating on tightening the string around their ankles. "If you tighten that any more, we aren't going to be able to feel our feet," she said in a hushed tone.

"Sorry, but I don't know how to make this better."

She knew he meant the thing between him and Erica, and not the string cutting the circulation of her foot off. Montana tried not to look at Erica, but she couldn't help herself. Erica caught her looking and glowered at her. Montana tried to let it slide by focusing on her group again, but there had to be a way to make this better. She caught App's eagle eye.

"You two 'bout ready to do this?" He hiked a bushy brow. "Ain't no call to get intimidated by a little unpleasantness."

He, of course, was talking loud enough to wake the dead. "App, behave," Luke muttered, looking perplexed by the entire issue.

"I am. The way I see it, we're all adults

here, and we can act like it." He looked sternly at Erica, reminding Montana of a school-teacher giving a child a warning in class for misbehavior.

Erica crossed her arms in a huff and glared at the cowboy sitting beside her. He was watching the minidrama unfolding in front of him with all the enthusiasm of a man about to get a healthy tooth pulled.

"Are you going to just sit there and let him talk to me that way?" she huffed.

The cowboy looked at her with a hint of humor in his eyes. "Hey, you're the one who threw tea all over Luke. Grow up, Erica." Without another word he dropped the string he was holding, tipped his hat and strode off. Fury destroyed Erica's face and she turned the color of an eggplant. She threw the sack down and stormed after the man who'd just humiliated her in front of everyone.

Luke had behaved like a perfect gentle-man.

Montana was impressed. As hard as Erica had pushed, he'd barely even voiced his frustration. It was far better than the way she'd have handled it. Yet she knew that was the Christian way to handle it. Though he didn't talk about his faith much, in small ways she saw how he lived it. It wasn't put on to impress others. It was a true faith, a quiet faith lived through character, honesty and trying to do the right thing.

Talk about getting the wrong impression of a person right from the get-go. Boy, had she done it.

The three-legged teams got downright rough when it came to winning. Montana soon learned that, before the next festival, she was going to have to practice if she wanted to make any kind of mark in the world of three-legged racing.

"I still can't believe we got whupped," Luke said, laughing as he and Montana made their way over to the cow chip throwing contest thirty minutes later.

"Well, the hop-'n'-run didn't work for us."

"But that wasn't all our fault. It was partly due to that other couple who tried out the maneuver, got tangled up and took us out."

"They did kind of resemble a bowling ball."

"And we were the pins."

"More like sitting ducks," Luke grumbled. "I still should have been able to get us up and make it across the finish line before we did. We got 'plum whupped' as App and Stanley would say. They were not too impressed with us." He chuckled so hard his shoulders shook. Looking at him she found herself smiling, too. It had turned into a great day.

Hooking her arm in his, she felt closer to him than she wanted to, but she wasn't worrying about it at the moment. Like he'd said earlier, she needed to relax where they were concerned.

"We did just fine," she said, then halted dead in her tracks at the cow chip competition. "Whoa, Nelly!"

The last thing she expected to see after they'd gotten whupped in the three-legged race was a line of women raring to throw cow chips! But there they were, lined up, studying the pile of chips, trying to figure out which one would fly the farthest. It was serious business.

"Looks like I have a little more competition here than just Lacy." She spotted Lacy and headed toward her. She was grinning and waving them over.

"Hey, just remember to be positive. A little can-do spirit and you've got this."

She rolled her eyes. "I think I've created a monster."

"Nope, I was like this before I met you."

"Oh, that's so good to know."

He threw an arm around her shoulder and pulled her close. Montana's stomach erupted in butterflies. She wasn't sure how much longer she could stop herself from falling for Luke.

The stands were full, and that put huge smiles on the matchmaking posse, as they worked the welcome station next to the entrance of the arena building. App and Stanley, along with Sam, were helping out at the booth, while Norma Sue's husband, Roy Don, was the announcer, and Hank, Esther Mae's husband, was helping work one of the gates. No doubt about it, they were all having a good time seeing familiar faces and reconnecting. It was part of the fun for all the older people of town, and Lacy was thrilled to be meeting them, too. She and Tate were acting as greeters. Last time Montana had glimpsed them, they'd been busy. This was why Montana was shocked when she saw Lacy come around the corner of the barn, where she and her horse were warming up before their barrel race. Lacy was clipping along just short of a run as she halted in front of Murdock.

"Looking good, Miss Queen of the Cow Chip Toss," she cooed, rubbing Murdock's forehead and grinning up at Montana.

"Thanks, Mrs. Barely Runner-Up." It had been big fun, and she'd only beaten Lacy by a nose. "I feel good. I'm hoping our good fortune in the cow-chip toss will continue on." Lacy's smile beamed up at her. "You can do it. You and Murdock are ready, and I know God's going to smile at your efforts."

"Thanks, Lacy, really. What are you doing out here? Don't they need your smiling face at the welcome table?"

She waved a dismissive hand. "Naw, I left little man Tate in charge for a few minutes. It's all good." She chuckled, then placed her hands on her hips and tilted her head. "I wanted to come out here and see you before your ride. Can you dismount and let's say a prayer?"

"Sure, I'd love to." The instant Montana's feet touched the ground, Lacy threw her arms around her.

"I love you, Montana! I just want you to know that. And I know, whatever happens out there, God's going to be with you. Win or lose, you've trained hard and given it your all, and you'll give God the glory. I feel it in my heart of hearts that you're going to do great. Yep, yep, yep, I do," she sang, grinning widely. Just the joyful sound of it made Montana feel positive and happy. "Now, let's talk to God, girlfriend."

Montana's heart was pounding as Lacy said a quick, heartfelt prayer for everyone's safety that night, and for victory for Montana, if it be God's will. After she finished, Montana hugged her tightly, holding on for a long moment. "Lacy, you don't know what coming here has meant to me. Thank you so much." She let go, but kept talking. "I was floundering in anger and bitterness when you reached out to me. You've helped me start finding myself again."

Lacy's brilliant blue eyes glowed with warmth as she smiled deep into Montana's. "I love you and I know you've still got a lot going on inside your heart. I know you're hurt and betrayed and all kinds of mixed-up things going on in there. I'm praying you give it all to God. Just give it to Him and let Him show you the freedom that comes from giving all your troubles over to Him. But right now, you have to focus. Let God help you do that, too. Now, get in the zone,"

Lacy grabbed her by the arms and turned her toward Murdock. "Get on this horse and then go out there and fly, baby, fly!"

Luke had a death grip on the rail as he watched for Montana and Murdock to step into position for the next run. Standing on an elevated walk beside the arena's chutes gave him the perfect vantage point to see both the arena floor and the alley where Montana would begin and end her run. He watched another rider as she and her horse made the last barrel and charged back toward the alley and the finish.

The times had been good tonight, and yet he knew if Montana was on her game she'd take it. But that required her focus, and he wasn't sure she was there. Not after their incident behind the popcorn stand earlier that afternoon. He was nervous as he waited for her turn to come up. Nervous knowing that if she didn't win, it could very well be his fault. He hadn't meant to cause a problem.

Roy Don called her name out over the loudspeaker, and Luke watched Montana move into position. He almost hunkered down so that she couldn't see him. He didn't want to distract her in any way. Then he realized how ridiculous that was. There was no way she could see him amid all that was around her. Thankfully, from the intense look on her face, she wasn't thinking about anything but the barrels. This was good. This was what she needed.

Murdock snorted, ready, his body quivered with the excitement and energy, waiting to explode out of the gate the instant he got the go-ahead.

"Settle down," Luke murmured, despite the fact that Montana couldn't hear him. "You've got this, Babe. You've got this." He said a silent prayer and his fingers tightened on the cold steel bar, felt it biting into his palms.

"Not nervous, are you, bro?" Jess asked, walking up to stand beside him. "Any tighter and you're going to bend that rail."

Luke acknowledged him but didn't spare him a glance, not wanting to miss the moment Montana charged the gate. "I want her to win."

Come on, girl, give your all. Focus. She was riding hard. Murdock was blazing. They kept their pattern close, Murdock dug in as tight as he could rounding the first barrel. He was so low as he made the turn that Montana was on the level with the barrel, her knee just missing it by a breath of air as they headed toward the second barrel.

"She's doing great," Jess said.

She was, and from somewhere in the stands he heard her name being yelled above the rising roar, as others realized they were seeing an extraordinary run. He knew Stanley was one of them, and Esther Mae, too. And others she'd touched in some way. As she rounded the last barrel, as clean and close as was possible, Luke's spine tingled. His fingers had welded themselves to the rail for life or he'd have jumped over the chute into the arena. Man, he was proud of her.

Her expression was totally intense, as she and Murdock moved as one at the speed of light toward the timing point. Relief hit him the instant she passed the mark and her unbelievable time clicked onto the reading.

"She did it!" he exclaimed, grinning like a kid with a new pony.

Jess grinned back. "Yeah, bro, she did it all right. Now, do you want to fess up and admit that there's a *little* more going on between the two of you than friendship?"

Montana's adrenaline was flowing like Niagara Falls when she hopped from her horse. She'd known, coming around the last barrel, that they'd done well. Her determined sweetheart of a horse had plunged forward with all the power he possessed, and laid it all out there as he raced for the time.

The instant she was out of the alley and clear of the other riders, she leaned forward and hugged Murdock's neck. "You did great!" If they lost tonight, it would be because someone else rode exceptionally well and deserved to win. Several other riders congratulated her on a good ride. She locked her arms around Murdock's neck and buried her face in his mane. Fighting to control her emotions, she said a prayer and praised God. They hadn't announced it yet, but she knew this had been the ride of a lifetime.

And all because of God and this amazing animal. "Thank you for not giving up on me," she whispered, talking to Murdock and God at the same time.

"Hey, cowgirl, good ride."

The sound of Luke's voice sent a thrill racing through Montana. She turned to find him smiling down at her. "Thanks! Did you see him?" she exclaimed, beaming from the inside out, so proud of Murdock she could burst. "What a champion. Murdock came through with flying colors." She patted him again and felt so proud, she knew she was glowing.

Luke laughed, stepped in and completely took her by surprise when he swung her into his arms, lifting her feet off the ground for a second. "You did okay yourself," he said, their mouths only inches away from each other as he looked into her eyes. "But I knew you would. I had every confidence in you."

Breathless, her arms around his neck, she tried to focus on what he was saying and not on how nice it felt to be wrapped in his arms, or that he was still holding her. She was beaming with joy and wishing he would kiss her. He believed in her! He had confidence in her. The idea was intoxicating. She remembered their first meeting and how he said she could ride. It felt good that he would be so sure of her.

"Th-thanks, Luke," she managed, knowing she should move out of his arms, but was unable to make her feet move. Everything around her seemed to fade into the background. They just stood there looking at each other, smiling.

The loudspeaker crackled to life. "It's official. Montana Brown is our top score in the women's barrel racing!"

The words rang out, reverberating through the building. Montana's heart jumped in her chest. "Yes!" she exclaimed, unable to believe that she'd won her first rodeo in years. She'd hoped for it, dreamed of it—and God had blessed her hard work. Her excitement was so great that she reacted without thought—okay, maybe there was a little thought. She engulfed Luke and kissed him.

Luke was kissing Montana. He'd wanted to kiss her the second he'd scooped her up, but he'd made himself behave. He'd been thinking about it though, and then he'd made himself let her go.

When she'd thrown her arms around him and kissed him, he'd responded automatically to the feel of her lips on his. Her arms held him tightly and their hearts were beating together. Tenderness surged inside him and he felt as if he'd found something he'd lost. He'd been tense the entire time she'd been riding, and Jess had been right when he said there was more here between them. He hadn't realized how much he was rooting for Montana.

How much he cared whether she still had what it took to pursue her dream.

He knew that she was kissing him purely out of excitement and celebration. A quick peck on the lips and a hurrah she'd won. But the instant her lips met his, Luke pulled her close and kissed her with feeling.

They heard the oohing and ahhing at the same moment.

"It's about time," Esther Mae cooed, as they broke apart to find the matchmakers grinning from ear to ear. Beside them stood App, Stanley, Sam and Lacy. They looked like they were watching the ending of a romantic chick flick.

And he and Montana were the stars!

Chapter Sixteen

"I think it's a blessing," Adela said, smiling gently at Montana. She was standing at the entrance of Murdock's stall with Esther Mae and Norma Sue.

"Your first rodeo in forever, and you win!" Esther Mae gushed, her green eyes flashing with excitement. "*And* you get the cowboy!"

Montana felt queasy. She really, really did.

"And at our first hometown rodeo. I'd call that a success," Norma Sue clapped her hand on Montana's back.

After being discovered kissing in the alley, Luke had quickly disengaged himself—he'd been polite, even joked a smidge—then disappeared. She'd done the same using Murdock as an excuse to head back to the stall.

She was brushing him down when the posse showed up blocking the stall entrance.

There was no way out. There was no escape. She was stuck while they discussed her as if she was part of the conversation. She wasn't, though; she hadn't said a word.

"Y'all," she said, pausing her brushing. "I hope y'all don't get your hopes up too high. Me and Luke are just friends."

Three sets of eyes looked at her like she was crazy.

"Friends?" Norma Sue grunted. Her white cowboy hat was pushed back on her head. Her kinky gray hair surrounded her head like a halo, as she looked skeptical. "That wasn't a friendly kiss."

"You can admit it," Esther Mae urged. "Love is a wonderful thing. You make such a sweet couple. My goodness, y'all took my breath away. It was just plumb beautiful."

Adela laid a gentle hand on Esther Mae's arm. "It's okay, Esther Mae. Maybe Montana needs a little time to adjust to the idea."

Esther Mae's eyes flashed wide-open. "Ohhh! That's right. It could have just snuck up on you. Swept you right off your feet in surprise. I mean, you did just win and all. Love blossoms in the midst of exciting moments."

Montana wasn't so sure about anything at

the moment. She didn't really want to think about it, standing here with all these eyes and hopes and wishes pinned on her like this. She wanted to go off and try to make some sense of all of this. She was overwhelmed. There was no doubt about that.

But she wasn't in love.

"Y'all, I just won my first rodeo. I'm planning on winning a whole lot more. And nothing is going to get in my way this time."

"That was uncomfortable."

Luke was standing at the back of the building. He could hear Roy Don's voice announcing the next event. He wasn't expecting company when his brother stepped around the corner. "You saw that, did you?"

Jess's forehead crinkled up. "Who didn't? You two were in sight of almost the entire arena. Or at least those who were behind the scenes."

"That's right," Colt said, poking his head around the corner. "I saw it from clean across the bull pens."

"When did you get in?" Luke asked. Colt looked tired. His eyes were weary, and he knew he'd been driving a long haul in order to make it in for this ride. Rodeo life wasn't easy. When you were going for the national level and the big money and fame, paying your dues was a strain on the best of them.

He jabbed his hands in his pockets and looked at the ground before bringing his gaze up to meet Luke's. "I just rolled in. I was checking out my ride when I heard them announce Montana's name. I just happened to glance in the direction of the alley when I saw you two have your little moment. Big brother, if you aren't into having your love life open and on the lunch plate special, I'd say cool it when you're in the public."

"Didn't do it on purpose. It just happened. And by the way, I wasn't the one who initiated that. Montana did and honestly, it was purely out of excitement of winning. Believe me, I know."

Jess let out a low whistle. "What news station you been watching? The broadcast I just got a few minutes ago said loud and clear that the woman was every bit as interested in that kiss as you were."

"I'm watching the same station you are, Jess. Maybe you need to tune your TV a little, Luke," Colt advised with a weary grin.

Luke knew they didn't mean anything by their teasing, but he wasn't feeling it at the moment. His thoughts were locked on Montana. What was she thinking right now?

She'd kissed him out of excitement. He knew it. Yes, there was that "thing" going on between them that she was so adamant about not wanting. And he understood why. She'd had her dreams put on hold for long enough. He'd seen her expression as she rode. He'd been watching her dedication for weeks now. There was no way she was letting anything get in the way of her dreams ever again. And this win…it cemented the deal. Nope, she didn't have to tell him that she wasn't interested in falling in love if it meant she couldn't devote all of her time to fulfilling that dream. "It doesn't matter what y'all saw. What matters is Montana won tonight. And that's just the beginning of the journey. She's about to hit the road just like you, Colt."

"If you want it bad enough, there's a way to make it all work." Jess was studying him with steady eyes.

"Yeah," Colt agreed. "I see fellas making it work out on the road. Sure, it's tough, but they tell me where there's love, there's a way."

"There you go. That 'bout sums it up right there. Montana Brown isn't going to let a little thing like love get in her way. Because she loved her dad, she put Murdock out to pasture and got a degree in accounting."

"Accounting? Montana?" Colt asked while Jess whistled. "That's the craziest thing I ever heard. No way she's an accountant."

"Not exactly a fit, is it?"

"Well, no. Nothing against accounting— but Montana looks like someone who'd have a career that involved something outdoors. Accounting's an office job. It just doesn't fit."

"No, it doesn't fit. Montana is an outdoors kind of gal. This is what she's meant to do. Just like you were meant to ride bulls, Colt."

Colt's eyes narrowed, and he rubbed the five o'clock shadow on his chin. "If you're right about that, then you might be in trouble, Luke."

Luke stared out across the darkness to where the Ferris wheel lit up the night. "Boy, don't I know it."

"You didn't make the posse too happy," Lacy said when Montana climbed into the stands to watch the bull riding event. It was late, but the stands were still packed. The bull riding was the main attraction. She hadn't seen Luke since their kiss, and she wondered where he'd gone to. Her stomach was a little queasy, thinking about the entire thing.

"I don't know what to say, Lacy." Tate was sleeping in his carrier, looking peaceful despite the ruckus going on around him. She studied him instead of looking at Lacy.

"I'm sorry all of this is getting in the way of your celebrating your win tonight."

Not exactly what she was expecting Lacy to say. "It's all right. I'm happy about the win. But I'm confused about everything else. Please don't tell anyone else though."

"I promise. I really am sorry. I want you to be happy, Montana. I'm so happy with Clint and Tate that I get a little pushy sometimes." She smiled. "You know me."

Montana laughed. "If you weren't jumping into things with both feet, then we'd all think something was wrong with you. I know your heart's in the right place. And I know that about the posse, too."

The arena was busy as the bull fighters got in place. A clown, not to be mistaken for the bull fighters, came out and started acting silly, running around and doing tricks and talking to the crowd. He'd been entertaining the crowd all night, but he was doing one last stint before the fighters took over.

"You'd probably make a great bull fighter if you wanted," she said, looking at Lacy. "You'd be good at rescuing people. I mean, that's what you did to me."

Lacy ran a hand through her tousled blond hair. "I don't know about that. I know I get folks into trouble sometimes. I hope I help them, though. You'd have been okay with or without me. You know that, don't you?"

"I'm finding my way, I think."

The bull riding had begun, and the first bull exploded from the gate with a wild twist that immediately had the rider flying to the ground. The bull fighters moved in, one dodging between the fallen rider and the bull, drawing the bull's attention as the other fighter moved in and helped the cowboy up and got him headed toward the fence. A bull fighter's job was one of the most dangerous jobs out there. These guys tonight were good and Montana hoped nothing bad happened. She was always worried during this event, always dreading the worst. She was relieved that it was starting out with the promise of a good night.

Lacy had stopped talking to watch also. Now that the danger was over, she looked at

Montana and asked, "Has that finding your way got a little to do with Luke?"

She couldn't deny it. She knew that somehow, spending time with him had helped her. "Yes, it does. Just getting to know him has helped me. The man has been through some tough times. And yet, he's mostly positive."

"He seemed that way to me. I don't know everything he's been through, but like Clint told you the other day, I know he's been working and saving since he was young. And I know his dad was a pretty bad alcoholic."

"I admire him. He's helped me think about things. Like not letting this anger at my dad eat me up. And when I'm really down on myself, he's been there to pick me up and tell me not to let it get to me." She thought about all the times that he'd helped her focus on her goals. She smiled, thinking about him.

"He sounds like a great guy." Lacy was watching her closely.

"He is," Montana admitted quietly.

"And what about that kiss?" Lacy asked, biting back a grin, her brows lifting expectantly.

Montana laughed, remembering. "You just couldn't help yourself, could you?"

"Nope. I couldn't. It was too good. You

should have seen the look on your face when you threw your arms around him."

"I was excited, Lacy. I'd just won my first rodeo," she said, defending her actions. "He was there, and I kissed him out of excitement."

Lacy smiled. "Whatever you say, it's your business. But something tells me you wouldn't have thrown your arms around just anyone and kissed him like you did Luke."

"You've got me there," Montana said, with a sheepish smile. There was no way around that one. "Lacy, to tell you the truth, I don't know what's going on. I think about him all the time. But I didn't come here to get involved with anyone. And I don't want to get involved with anyone. But that doesn't stop the fact that, when he's around—or even when he isn't—I think about him. The man just does something to me, and I don't seem to be able to stop it. And I just don't know what in the world I'm going to do about it."

Lacy was beaming at her. "Relax, girl-friend. You're in love."

Montana shook her head in vigorous denial. "No, I'm not."

"You can deny it all you want, but I'm telling you it's true."

"Then I'll just get right out of love. I've got plans. I've got things I need to do—barrel races I have to win and points I have to gain in order to make it to the finals. I do not have time to fall in love."

She was not in love.

She wasn't. No way. No how.

Just as she was in the middle of her internal argument, she saw Luke walk out onto the elevated metal walkway that connected the chutes where the bull riders climbed down and settled onto the backs of their rides. Luke was walking beside a bull rider. The man was not as tall as Luke, but he had the same swagger that Luke had. Though she couldn't see his face because of the protective facemask that he wore, she knew without doubt that this must be the younger brother, Colt.

"Is that Colt that Luke just came out with?"

"Yes, that's him. You haven't met him, have you?"

"No." As of yet, she hadn't met Colt. Luke spoke to the cowboy, placed his hand on his back and bowed his head briefly. They looked like they were saying a prayer. When it was done, the cowboy, Colt, climbed over the side of the chute. Looking at Luke, he then eased himself down onto the restless bull's back. Montana held her breath. Luke and Clint were gripping Colt's protective vest—the vest was to protect his chest from the bull's horns, and Clint and Luke were there to help the rider get out of the chute in case the bull went wild in the close confines of the chute. The rider could be harmed easily if he was trapped or slipped between the bull and the gates. Montana held her breath.

"This always makes me nervous," she said.

"Me, too," Lacy agreed, tapping her fingers on the metal bench. "I don't want to see someone get hurt. But from what I understand, Colt is really good."

The gate was pulled open and the bull blasted from the chute, twisting and turning and kicking like he was the meanest, orneriest bad boy around. And Colt held on! It was a wild ride. But Colt held his seat on its back. He was on at the end of a great eight-second ride! "Wow, that was awesome." Montana admired his style and smiled when he jumped from the bull's back, waved to the crowd, dodged the angry bull and jogged to the fence, scaling it like he was out for a Sunday afternoon stroll.

Lacy laughed. "He's a little cocky, wouldn't you say?"

"Just a little. But I guess if you're that good, you can be," Montana said, thinking about all the time he spent working in order to qualify for the nationals. It was something she and Murdock were about to begin.

"Fans enjoy seeing some personality from the riders," Lacy said.

Luke met Colt coming over the fence and gave him a high-five and a back slap. He was all smiles as they stood there. Looking at him, her heart had begun thundering louder than if she'd been the one riding the bull. Luke Holden was a threat to her dream. The idea sent a chill racing down her spine. She didn't want to be in love. She didn't want to worry about trusting a man.

No, what she needed was to focus. And stay focused, if she wanted to have any chance of making her dream a reality.

"Lacy," she said, taking action. "I'm going for it."

Serious blue eyes met hers. "It's time."

Luke's words of encouragement came to mind. He'd told her God had given her a special talent. He'd been so confident in her all along.

"Yes. It's something I have to do." She thought about it for a moment, then decided to say it. "I believe God gave me this talent and He has a purpose for me in doing it." Luke's words echoed again. "I can't let it go to waste another day."

"You know you can help out with Tate as long as you want."

"I know, and I love it. But I think I'm going to need something else on the side to help with all the expenses. Unless I start out winning money, I won't be able to last long."

"The old saying, 'where there's a will, there's a way,' comes to mind. You've got the will, and if it's in God's plan, He'll make the way."

Montana knew in order for her to reach the National Final Rodeo Championship, it would take a miracle and thousands of miles hauling and racing time. It would take money and commitment and it would be harder for her than most because she would be doing it on her own.

Montana wondered if she was biting off more than she could handle. She sighed as her gaze settled on Luke, leaning on the fence, talking with a group of cowboys and watching the bull riding. Her heart clutched inside her chest and again his words encouraged her. She knew he'd tell her she could do this, and even more, she knew he'd tell her to go for it.

Chapter Seventeen

Montana couldn't sleep. She finally got out of bed around five, after staring at the ceiling for hours. She took a shower, got dressed, then quietly padded through the house with her boots in her hand. Outside, she sat down on the deck steps and tugged her boots on. The sun was just coming up and she wanted to be riding before others were stirring.

She needed space. Time to think and be totally alone.

Time to pray. She closed her eyes and let the calm of the early morning seep in around her. The air had the scent of fresh hay. She inhaled and asked God to guide her because she needed him desperately.

She needed help getting her life figured out. She needed some peace in her heart and in her head, and she wasn't getting it. Even the rodeo win hadn't helped. The satisfaction that she'd hoped to find with the win wasn't coming. Yes, she'd been excited—she'd shown that when she threw her arms around Luke—but peace? Nope, there had only been more confusion.

She'd thought when she talked to Lacy about starting her quest by hitting the rodeo trail that she'd feel some kind of satisfaction, but she didn't. All she felt was a heavy heart. All her life she'd wanted to be a cowgirl, and now here was her shot. Why couldn't she be happy?

Across the pasture she could see the shadow of where the festival trailers and booths were set up. But other than the soft bark of a dog in the distance, all was quiet. It was different from the way it had been last night, or would be later that day. One thing was certain, the first night of the rodeo had been a big success.

She was walking toward the arena when she heard Samantha let out a lonesome *heehaw,* as if the little donkey had heard her approaching and was begging for some company. Instead of going to the arena where Murdock's stall was, she walked across the gravel to the barn. The smell of fresh hay filled the air as she entered. Immediately, Samantha hee-hawed again.

"Hold your horses," Montana said, striding toward the back of the stalls. The low lights illuminated the area well and Montana had no trouble seeing that the little donkey had been busy. The wooden bar they'd used to secure the gate better had been worked halfway out of its slot. Batting her big brown eyes at Montana, Samantha curled her plump lips back and gave a grin.

Montana was tickled at the sight. "Are you proud of yourself?" she asked through her chuckles. "If I'd have been out here a little later, you would have been free, and then where would we be?"

"From what I hear, she'd have let all the livestock out and enjoyed it," Luke said from behind her.

Montana whirled around. "What are you doing here?"

He shrugged. "I couldn't sleep. And I've been a little bit worried about Samantha getting loose and causing problems. So I decided to head over here and make sure things were secure."

Montana stuffed her hands in her pockets.

"This donkey must really be good to have y'all so worried."

"I had visions of driving up and seeing my livestock running free while everyone was asleep."

Montana grimaced. "That wouldn't be good." She was so glad to see him. It was all she could do not to go over and hug him…but that wasn't what she needed to do. She didn't want to get involved. *You* are *involved.*

She knew she was on the verge of falling hard for the cowboy if she didn't watch herself extremely carefully. That meant not throwing herself at him.

Instead, she glanced down at the donkey who still had her head stuck through the bars of the gate. She batted her eyes and curled her lips back, exposing her big-toothed grin again. "Is this donkey human or what? She smiles like she knows what I'm thinking."

Luke chuckled and moved to stand beside her. "Maybe she does. A donkey is a very perceptive animal."

Luke stood close to her, his arm almost touching hers. It was like torture. Why did he have to stand right there? Didn't he know she was having trouble controlling herself? Probably not.

"I'm going to say that she was probably thinking you have a lot on your mind," he said quietly as he reached out and rubbed Samantha's nose. The little burro closed her eyes and breathed heavily—like a sigh.

Montana was almost jealous.

"How would she know this?" she asked, realizing what he'd said.

"She could tell, because you came to the barn so early. She would also think you're thinking about all the things you're going to have to do to get ready to hit the road for qualifying."

So the man had her figured out. "Think you're pretty smart, don't you?" she asked, sliding a look his way.

"Me? Nah, I'm just saying what Samantha is thinking. But if I was the one who was perceptive, I'd say you had a certain cowboy on your mind, too. And you were probably beating yourself up about kissing him last night."

Her heart was thumping like a rabbit running for its life. In a way that's how Montana felt, too. Looking at Luke, she saw how easily she could forgo her dreams and settle for a life right here with him. Be content like Lacy was with her home and family. She could love Luke.

"You have a high opinion of yourself, don't you?" she teased, but it wasn't easy to do.

He leaned against the gate so that he was looking at her. "You know me and Samantha are right about everything about you."

She laughed. "And just how are y'all so sure?"

"For starters, it is five in the morning. That's awful early for you to be out. I'd say that spells sleeplessness."

"What about the kiss?"

"Ahh, the kiss," he drawled, giving her a slow, toe-curling smile. "That was actually wishful thinking on my part." He lifted a hand to touch a strand of hair that was hanging over her shoulder. He slowly wound it around his finger, staring at it before lifting his beautiful brown eyes to hers. "I've been thinking about that kiss ever since it happened. I tried to distract myself from it all night, during the rest of the rodeo, but it didn't help. You—and that kiss—were on my mind the whole time. And then I couldn't sleep. I guess a tiny part of me was hoping you hadn't just kissed me because of the win."

She was toast!

Done. Stick a fork in her.

The sigh came out, despite all efforts to keep her head.

The guy was just plain irresistible. She took a step toward him. He opened his arms, and the next thing she knew, his arms were around her and they were kissing. The feel of his lips was firm yet tender as he kissed her. Pulling away slightly, he searched her stunned and confused eyes before lowering his lips to hers again. It was as if she'd been waiting all of her life for this moment. For the feel of this man's lips to connect with hers, for his heart to connect with hers.

He broke the kiss and laid his forehead against hers. Everything faded away in that instant. Her head was quiet. Her heart was calm.

Montana could have stayed like that forever.

"I can't get you off of my mind, Montana. I'm sorry." He sighed. "I know I've been trying to keep this simple. But it's complicated."

"Boy, don't I know it," she said, nodding her head against his. His arms tightened around her and at some point hers had wrapped around his neck.

He looked about as serious as a man in a face-off with a rattlesnake. "Montana, I came here to ask you to go to dinner with me. It's time for you to go out with me. Yes, I know it will cause rumors—but with that kiss last night getting full coverage by one and all, everyone knows there's a little something going on between the two of us."

"Yes, I think you're right."

"I know I am. You can just—wait, you said yes, I was right? Does that mean you're saying yes to dinner?"

Her lip twitched with a smile she couldn't contain. It was adorable. He was flustered. "I meant yes on both counts. Dinner would be wonderful. And long overdue."

"Did you hear that, Samantha? You're my witness," Luke said, looking at the little burro. She laid her bulbous nose against Luke's hip and snorted.

Montana and Luke laughed, and as if knowing she'd done something good, Samantha snorted again, pulled her head from between the rails and let out a long *hee-haw*.

"Tell me about it, Samantha. We should have come to you a long time ago so you could set us straight." Luke gave Montana a nod and tugged her close again. "Yup. We might all be getting on the same page, finally."

Samantha pranced around her stall, her tail lifted out and her head held high. She looked as if she was about to bust out in dance as she batted her eyes at them.

"That is one funny donkey." Montana chuckled.

Luke looked down at her and cocked a brow. "That is one smart little gal, is what she is."

"I wonder." Montana sighed, leaning her head against Luke's shoulder. "What her advice would be on something else I have going on in my life?"

"I don't know, darlin', but you hang with me and I promise you we'll get whatever's bothering you all figured out." He kissed her forehead and rubbed her shoulder. "I promise, I'll help you, and so will God."

Montana breathed in slowly. There was a mixture of excitement and comfort in his arms. Of anticipation for the step they were taking. And worry of what it could bring.

Worry and joy, too, but for now, there was comfort and peace.

And the gentle touch of a very special man's hand.

"27"

Sem mil cot agood agonds her will see and bette so and then aged both light. She to need Aard se puts phone to bath on on shines on off raised her open at then.

Chapter Eighteen

"Yoo-hoo! Montana." Esther Mae waved from her position at the top of the Ferris wheel.

"Stop waving, Esther Mae," Norma Sue barked. From where Montana and Luke stood, waiting in line to get on the ride, it was clear that Norma Sue was white as a sheet. Her hands were glued to the protective bar. "Can't you see this thing is moving every time you do that?"

"Norma Sue, are you afraid of heights?" Luke called, tipping his Stetson back so he could see her better.

"Yes, she is," Esther Mae called for all to hear. "I practically had to drag her on here with me. Look, Norma Sue, it rocks." The redhead moved side to side, living dangerously when Norma Sue elbowed her in the ribs.

"You just wait till I get my boots back on the ground. I'm going to get you."

"She better have her running shoes on," Montana said.

"I wouldn't want to tangle with Norma Sue when she's out for payback," Luke said.

"Esther!" Norma Sue squealed, and Esther Mae hooted with laughter.

Luke laughed. "You sure you want to get on this thing? It does wobble a lot!"

"Are you afraid of heights, too?"

"Even if I am, I'd risk it to get to ride it with you. I was just worried about your safety."

She patted his arm. "I'll be fine. And don't you worry, big guy, I'll take good care of you up there."

He hugged her and she slipped her arm around his waist. Standing arm in arm with him, they watched the buggy with Esther Mae and Norma Sue lower a little more, as each car between them and the ground emptied out. Montana was living dangerously, knowing they'd spotted Luke's arm across her shoulders. But she didn't care.

"Glad that's over with," Norma Sue said, relief surging in her voice. "Y'all sure you want to go up in that bag of nuts and bolts?"

"We're going," Luke assured her.

"That's a good place for y'all to go. Have a good time," Esther Mae said. "And just don't pay Norma Sue no mind. She had fun. She's just too stubborn to admit it."

Luke leaned close and whispered in her ear as they were leaving. "Did you catch how sly they were being about my arm being around you?"

"Yes, they don't want to mess up a good thing."

He helped her into the buggy and then sat down beside her, immediately placing his arm across the seat behind her. "I don't want to mess anything up, either."

Montana breathed the cotton candy-scented air and let herself enjoy the ride. "It would be wonderful if life could be as carefree as this feels," she said, as they reached the top of the wheel and were looking down on all the people milling around below.

"Yeah, from up here it feels removed from all that down there."

She smiled, her thoughts traveling to all that she'd pressed to the back of her mind. "The problem is, it's an illusion. All my problems are still waiting for me when I get back down." Why was she going there, when everything had been so perfect? She was with the perfect guy, on a perfect day, and she was opening her big mouth.

"True, but I can tell you, anything can be overcome."

She looked at him as the wheel swept them under before sending them back up to the top again. Anything can be overcome. Montana wasn't so sure.

The first of three Mule Hollow Homecoming Rodeos was a success. On both nights, they'd introduced all former residents who'd come home for the event. There had been several families who'd moved away, children all grown-up, some single and some with families of their own, coming back to show their kids where they'd once lived.

They all enjoyed remembering the town when it was a thriving oil town. They'd been sad when their parents had moved away to find work after the oil boom busted and all the work had dried up in Mule Hollow.

Sunday morning, the church lawn was filled with talk of the weekend. It was a roaring success.

Esther Mae and Norma Sue looked like they could fly they were so happy. Esther

Mae especially, since the summer hat that she wore was covered in feathers. Feathers that fluttered with every bob her head made as she talked nonstop about the festival.

Everyone was in an exceptionally good mood. Montana listened and took all the congratulations on her win. Everyone wanted to know what she was going to do next, and she told them she was going to hit the road for more rodeos the following week.

It seemed strange to her that she would actually be starting her lifelong dream. She was going to find another part-time job in addition to her helping out with Tate, and then she would just pray that she'd start winning. The money would help pay her way, or she wouldn't be able to make it. There was a lot of wear and tear that went along with hauling. There would be travel expenses, and then upkeep expenses on the truck and trailer, which Clint was lending her, and of course vet bills and entry fees. The list went on and on. It wasn't cheap shooting for the National Rodeo Finals in Las Vegas. Being one of the top fifteen in money and points was no easy feat. It was one thing to dream about it and another to take it on.

But that was exactly what Montana planned to do.

And if she was committing, she was committing one hundred percent.

She and Luke had talked a little about it the day before. After they'd gotten off the Ferris wheel, they'd hung out together some and talked about her riding. She'd told him of her decision to find another part-time job, and he'd told her he thought that was a good idea—until she started winning the big money and went full-time. She still smiled at the conviction in his voice. He hadn't been saying that to make her feel better; he'd been saying it because he really did think she would do well. The very idea had her waiting anxiously to see his smiling face come striding across the parking lot.

He didn't make it until the last song was being sung, just before Chance got up to preach. When the door opened, Montana glanced over her shoulder and her heart did the now familiar happy thump. As if their eyes were connected by a beacon, he zeroed in on her instantly, and strode straight up the aisle and scooted into the seat beside her.

Adela's piano playing seemed to pick up the pace, drawing Montana's gaze to find the delicate lady's blue eyes beaming from around the corner of the music sheet. And up in the choir loft, Esther Mae's and Norma Sue's smiles seemed to merge together, they were so huge.

Whether she wanted it or not, there was no denying that they had a successful match on the mind. Montana tried not to think about it. She tried to think only of enjoying his company. No strings attached. There had been nothing said, no indication that things were any different with her than with any of the other women he'd dated.

And she was fine with it. They were going out to dinner that evening and she'd teased him. Funny, she wondered if these butterflies and sick stomach were what all the others had felt.

As they sat beside each other, he closed the hymnal and placed it in the holder on the back of the pew in front of them. "You doing good this morning?" he asked as he leaned back beside her.

"Good," she said, listening to Pastor Chance's opening statement about the rodeo and festival. "How about you?"

He grinned. "I'm great. I've got a date tonight with a beautiful woman. What's not to be happy about?" His smile was as dazzling as his words, and it felt crazy wonderful, knowing he was talking about her.

Looking at him, Montana was very aware that Luke made her feel like a woman…and she loved it. It caused her to long for things she hadn't thought about in a long time.

Whistling a happy tune, Luke jogged down the steps and over to his truck. Tossing the keys into the air, he caught them on a flip and grinned. He was feeling good. He had a date with Montana Brown.

He had a surprise for her tonight, and he hoped she'd take him up on it. He had thought all afternoon about it, and felt like this was the perfect solution to her problem. Dinner was the perfect place to tell her, but he was a little worried about how she'd handle it.

He couldn't get to her house quick enough. He felt like a schoolboy on his first date. He'd been smiling all afternoon and was still smiling when he knocked on her door.

"Come in, come in," Lacy said, opening the door wide when she saw him. She was holding Tate as she beckoned him in. "I've been pacing the floors, waiting for the clock to hit six and for you to drive up. Yep, it's true, I think I may be more excited about you two going out than y'all."

"I hope not. I was kind of hoping Montana was excited. I know I am."

Lacy chuckled. "That's exactly the answer I wanted to hear. If you weren't excited, I'd think something was wrong with you. Clint had a call from one of his ranch hands that a cow was down so he had to go check on it, or he'd be here to see y'all off."

"Hey," Montana said, coming into the room. Her glistening dark hair was down around her shoulders tempting him to touch it. She wore a frilly white blouse with dressy jeans, and with the sparkle in her eye, she took his breath away. "Has Lacy given you the third degree? Has she made sure you understand that my curfew is ten sharp, and I must be home then or I'll be grounded for life, and never ever get to go out with you again?"

"Ha!" Lacy said. "I was just about to."

Luke chuckled. "I'm game for whatever Lacy throws at me. Whatever it takes to get this dinner date, I'll do."

Montana smiled. Her big eyes were bright with what he hoped was excitement about him being there. His heart was pounding in his chest, looking at her. And it was like nothing he'd ever experienced before. Everything had faded away and all he saw was her.

"I don't have any questions. You two crazy kids need to just get on out of here." Lacy's teasing words broke the moment, reminding Luke that he'd spoken to her before he'd gotten caught up in the unchartered feelings Montana evoked inside of him.

He'd had his hat in his hand ever since he'd rung the doorbell, and now tapped it lightly to his hip. "Then are you ready?" he asked.

"Yes she is," Lacy said, giving Montana a little nudge.

A few minutes later they were trucking down the road toward Ranger. He couldn't explain how happy he was as they drove the seventy miles to the closest large town near Mule Hollow. On the way they talked about various aspects of the festival and rodeo. He'd made reservations at a restaurant that overlooked a lake. He'd never been there before, but had heard it was nice, and he'd decided that he wanted to take Montana somewhere he'd never been before. He thought Montana was special, and he wanted this date to be special, too. He wanted Montana not to feel like just one of many women he took to dinner.

"This is beautiful," she said as the hostess led them to a table on the deck beside the water. A swan was floating in the water as Luke held Montana's chair out for her. She looked over her shoulder at him and smiled. Luke froze. He could live forever with that smile directed at him.

The idea was a sobering one.

"Luke, are you all right?" she asked, when he didn't scoot the chair up for her to sit in.

"Yeah," he said, jolted by the thoughts racing through his mind and the sudden longing tugging at his heart. What was happening with him? "Yeah, I'm good. Just thinking—Montana, you have the most beautiful smile I've ever seen."

She laughed as she sat down. "I'm sure you say that to all the girls."

He shook his head. "No, Montana, I don't. I'm telling you that your smile is the most beautiful I've ever seen." It was important for her to understand he was serious, and not just saying the words.

Her smile was genuine as he sat down across from her. "Thank you. I like that," she said quietly. "Whew, I'm a little nervous."

He reached across the table and laid his hand over hers, where she was picking at the edge of her napkin. "I'm nervous too." He held her unconvinced gaze. "Why don't we both take a breath and relax."

She nodded and breathed in. "Sounds like a good idea. I wasn't expecting to feel like a girl on her first date."

"I like the idea of that. I feel like a boy on his first date."

Their confessions made them laugh as the waitress came. By the time she left to fill their order, they'd both relaxed somewhat. Luke knew in his heart that this was a life-changing experience. Looking across the candlelit table at her, he knew he was feeling happy. And he liked it. Three weeks ago he wouldn't have believed it was possible. But that was before Montana Brown had ridden into his life.

Chapter Nineteen

The meal had been the most romantic meal Montana had ever had. The gentle lapping of the water against the deck, the soft moonlight that seemed to hover over the lake just for them. The swan gliding about on the water beside them added to the romance, along with the music that drifted lightly on the breeze to them. There was so much that made the night special, but it was the look in Luke's eyes that had her heart fluttering from moment to moment. The light touch of his hand when he'd grasped hers. And his words left her feeling like she was floating on cloud nine.

This was what falling in love was like... would be like, if it was happening to her.

When they were leaving the restaurant,

Luke took her hand in his. "Would you like to walk along the lake path for a little while?"

The warmth of his hand felt so nice. She nodded. "I'd like that."

They headed to the side of the restaurant and down to the pier. There was a sidewalk that led along the edge for a distance, past benches that had been placed along the way, and they followed it. Ahead of them, several yards away, an older couple strolled hand in hand, enjoying the night. They paused in a shadow and the woman placed her hand on the man's cheek. He bent and kissed her. A tug of emotions washed through Montana as she watched them. How many years had they been together? They could easily be newly-weds, or they could have been married for fifty years. Either way, just the sweetness of the gesture inspired her.

Looking up, she found Luke watching her. "I love that," she said, waving toward the couple as they disappeared.

His expression was thoughtful. "Makes you wonder what their story is, doesn't it?" He pulled her toward him.

Still holding his hand, Montana went willingly, her heart stopping, then it started racing. She felt off-balance. Luke Holden did that, set her world tilting.

"Yes, it does." She forced her voice to work as her gaze rested on his lips.

He lowered his head slightly, looking into her eyes as he paused mere inches from her. "You shake my world up, Montana," he murmured, and then kissed her.

The night was still, peaceful, easy. The instant his lips met hers, everything stopped, and she knew she was in danger. So many emotions she'd never experienced came into play in his arms. Her heart sighed and she felt as if she could stay there forever. As if God were smiling down on her.

Was this love?

There were so many reasons why she didn't want to fall in love. But she had.

How had this happened? In his arms, the walls she'd built around her heart seemed to crumble. She pushed gently on his chest and he pulled away, looking as stunned as she felt. Letting go of her, he walked a few feet, studying the moonlit water.

"Montana, I…"

Neither of them had been looking for anything serious, and yet they seemed on a collision course toward it. Was he feeling the same? Was that what had him turning his back on her?

"Montana, I've fallen in love with you."

His words took her breath away, even though she'd been wondering if it was possible that he could be feeling what she was feeling.

"No," she said, saying the first thing that came to her. "No, Luke." She paced to the water's edge, and it was her turn to stare out across it, with everything inside of her clashing. "I don't want to fall in love and neither do you. Remember, this was all just an infatuation and a friendship. It's not love. You don't want that. You want to get your ranch up and successful before you think about a marriage and a family. And I—" She slapped a hand to her chest. "I'm going on the rodeo circuit. I don't have time to think about being in love—"

That slow smile of his spread with maddening beauty across his face, lighting his eyes with humor. "Montana, it's true I wasn't looking for this. But it's also true that it's happened. Are you telling me that what I'm feeling from you isn't true?"

She glared at him. "You...you've taken a perfectly good evening and ruined it."

His eyes were twinkling with mirth. "Montana, it's going to be okay. I wasn't expecting this any more than you were, but I love you, and there isn't anything I can do about it but tell you."

"Well, don't sound so enthusiastic." She tried to think. Tried to figure this out.

He laughed. "Hey, I'm just being honest." He pulled her into his arms again.

"Montana, I've been feeling something inside myself, since knowing you, that I've never felt before. I feel joy every time I see you. And it runs deep and strong. I'm praying you'll see it, too."

"We haven't even finished our first date," she protested.

His grin widened. "I know a good thing when I see it, and you're the best thing I've ever seen. Montana, the first time I saw you racing around that barrel at Lacy's, I felt drawn to you. I wasn't expecting it to be more than a passing attraction, but there was no shaking it. One date, two, fifty. It doesn't matter, I'm in love with you."

She backed away from him. "I'm going on the rodeo circuit, Luke."

He stepped toward her and cupped her face. "Yes, you are. Nothing I'm saying is changing that. I'm just telling you that I love you, and I want a life with you. I want to raise babies with you and watch them grow up on the ranch."

Montana felt dazed. He was trying to sweep her off her feet. There couldn't be any sweeping going on right now. She had to focus. And she had to focus *now*.

And not on Luke. *No*. The only male she needed in her life right now was Murdock.... "I need to go home," she said. "I need to go home now."

Heart pounding, she ran back to Luke's truck.

Monday came bright and early. Montana woke up and saw Lacy and Tate sitting on the bed looking at her.

"So, how was it?" Lacy asked, grinning like a sly cat.

Montana rolled away from her and covered her head with her pillow. She hadn't slept at all, or at least she hadn't felt like she did until Lacy woke her. The last time she'd remembered staring at the clock, it had been 4:30 a.m. "What time is it?" she asked from beneath the pillow.

"Six. Me and Tate couldn't wait for you

to get up. The little fella is just a Curious George when it comes to knowing what's going on in his aunt Monty's love life."

Montana groaned. "It was a disaster."

"What happened?"

Montana yanked the pillow from her head and sat up, staring at Lacy in disbelief. "He told me he loved me! That's what."

"Woo-hoo!" Lacy exclaimed, clapping Tate's hands between hers and bouncing him on her lap. "We knew it! We knew it, didn't we, Tater!" Tate was grinning, his little mouth wide-open and his eyes bright. "Hold it." Lacy stopped midexclamation point. "What did you tell him?"

Montana was still reeling. "I told him we hadn't even finished our first date."

Lacy gasped while making an are-you-crazy face. "Montana, y'all have too been on dates. Maybe not technically, but you've had dinner here. And then there was the barbecue. And all that time at the arena. Oh, and going to put the fire out. Y'all have spent lots of time getting to know each other—"

"None of those were dates."

"You're being technical again. You've spent time with him. Don't forget all the time in the arena and the festival. You know there is something special there. I see those blue-green eyes of yours go dreamy when he enters the room."

Montana's stomach did somersaults. She'd thought about her feelings all night. It had been a quiet trip home, both of them tangled up in their own thoughts. She'd wondered what he was thinking of her reactions. There was no denying that she was crazy about him and that she had never felt with anyone the way she felt when she was around him.

Love. Yes, the emotion had actually entered her thoughts last night, too. But she couldn't believe it. It was irresponsible—she actually heard her father saying the words in her head, as she'd gone over and over her feelings toward Luke.

"How could he love me so soon?"

Lacy's expression was still stuck in a smile. "God has a way of letting hearts speak to each other. Don't get me wrong, I believe in knowing what you're doing. Yep, there is nothing worse than a woman letting a man sweet-talk her into making a bad mistake. But I do believe that some love happens quickly and some love grows slowly. To each his own love journey. You aren't denying your feelings because of your dad, are you?"

"Maybe in a way," Montana said. "I loved my daddy. Trusted him. Lacy, have you ever found out that the one person in all the world who you thought was most honorable and upright was a liar? That's what I did. And worse, I gave up my dreams for him." Her stomach lurched.

Lacy patted her knee. "I can't imagine how that must feel."

Montana hugged her pillow, watching Tate as he played with his momma's necklace. "I feel like such a whiner. I'm an adult. I am a CPA—whether I like it or not. I'm a strong, independent woman and I'm acting like a baby. I hate this."

Lacy was studying her with thoughtful eyes. "Do you love Luke?"

Montana buried her face in her pillow. "I think I do," she said, her voice muffled in the pillow. "But I can't," she said, sighing.

"The romantic in me is thrilled and happy and wants you to go throw yourself into his arms and let's have a wedding." Lacy laid her hand on hers. "But this is what I'm going to do. I'm going to continue to pray. I know God has a plan. He always does." She nodded her head enthusiastically when Montana frowned. "I think y'all go together like pie and ice cream."

"Only you would think that way," Montana said, her lip twitching despite her misery.

"There's no rush on this. Take it one day at a time. Just do me a favor and don't close your heart to this wonderful man God has put in your path, simply because your dad messed up. God can mend all fences and bring good from all things bad. Life is full of bad things. Wrongdoings and devastating blows. But God is always, always, always steady as the rock that He is. He will never leave you or forsake you, and He will not give you more than you can handle." Lacy rattled off promises from God like she was really expecting them to come true. "And I'm telling you that, in the process, He's making you stronger than you ever thought you could be."

Montana thought of Luke and all he'd been through as a kid growing up, and the man he'd become. She admired him so very much. Talk about strong. He was amazing. There was so much he could have held against God, and his mother and his dad. But he didn't seem to. It was something she longed to understand.

Montana took a deep breath. There were

so many things going on in her life. So many conflicts swirling around in her head and heart that she felt dizzy. "I'm not going to think about any of that today. Today, I'm going to make a plan before I hit the road hard."

"I told Clint yesterday to get the trailer and truck ready because you were about to shoot for the stars. You deserve it."

Did she? Montana knew the anger that was still bolted inside her heart. Luke had somehow dealt with issues of his own, and she wanted to know how he'd done it. Her heart hadn't softened, and it wasn't because she hadn't prayed about it. She had.

She wondered what Luke would think of her if he knew exactly how angry she was inside? He was the honorable one, she wasn't so honorable.

How could she feel so angry and then feel so guilty for not being able to forgive her dad?

She was just one goofed-up cookie, was all there was to it. God was probably looking down, wagging His head and wondering if she was ever going to get things figured out.

Montana wondered that, too.

* * *

"Luke, we came to talk."

It was practically the break of dawn, and the matchmaking posse was standing on Luke's front porch a couple of days after he and Montana had gone out. He pulled the door open, and there they stood with the rising sun at their backs. The roosters had barely stopped crowing it was so early.

"Okay. Shoot." He stepped back and motioned them to come inside.

Norma Sue led the way inside, barreling past him to stand beside the kitchen counter. Esther Mae and Adela followed. They were a work in contradictions as they passed him one by one. Norma Sue in her jeans and button-down shirt, topped off with her white Stetson, Esther Mae in her grape slacks and orange shirt that fought hard with her red hair. And then refined Adela, petite and fragile in her pale pink blouse and cream slacks. She gave him a lovely smile as she entered.

"We are so glad we caught you before you started your day," she said, patting his arm. "We know how busy you are."

He gave a wary smile, feeling oddly nervous with them looking like they were on official business. Matchmaking business, he presumed.

"We've come to ask you a favor." Norma Sue crossed her arms, looking like she dared him to say no. Luke knew she was like a steamroller when she got going, and he wondered if he was about to get mowed down.

"You know I'll do my best to help y'all any way I can." It was true. He loved and respected these ladies—despite being a bit scared of them. What were they up to?

"We think you should ask Montana to work for you," Esther Mae proposed, looking as if she'd just told him he'd won a million dollars.

He laughed because he'd already thought of the same thing. "You do? And what makes you think that?"

"We overheard Jess telling Sam that the business was growing and that you had been thinking about hiring some bookkeeping help."

He had been thinking that. He'd even thought about offering it to Montana last night, but then he'd gone and opened his big mouth and told her he loved her.

If he wanted to scare her off, he'd chosen exactly the right thing to say.

She'd almost run the seventy miles home from Ranger that night.

Offering the job to her might have put the last nail in his coffin, so he'd kept his mouth shut on the way home. "I've thought about it," he admitted to the ladies. "But I'm not so sure she would accept it. She—" He halted, the temptation to tell them he loved her churned inside of him.

"Why'd she get mad at you?" Norma Sue asked, studying him like a hawk.

Luke pulled at his collar. "I, ah—"

"You told her you loved her!" Ester Mae yelped. "Is that it?"

His mouth fell open. Instantly, three sets of eyes flew wide.

"Well, I'll be," Norma Sue hooted, slapping him on the back. "I'm impressed with you, Luke. You've got gumption."

"I didn't say—"

Adela smiled. "You don't have to explain. We're on your side."

Looking at their smiling faces, he caved. "I'm afraid I may have done more harm than good. She's not too happy about all of this.

I'm afraid offering her a job might do more harm than good. She might not take it."

Esther Mae harrumphed. "Are you kidding? She'll accept. She wants to rodeo and this is right up her alley."

"Not to mention she'd get to be near you in the bargain," Norma Sue added, her plump cheeks shining, she was grinning so big.

Luke stared at the ladies. He needed any and all the help he could get. He'd planned on offering her the job because it would be perfect for her and help him out, too, both in the business and personally, since it would give him an excuse to see her.

Adela had said little as Esther Mae and Norma Sue rattled on about all the positives of the situation. Their excited chattering was neverending. Miss Adela was watching him with her wise blue eyes, so sure and steady that he felt certain that this was the move to make. She didn't have to say anything, just be there, giving him that look.

"I'll ask her," he said at last.

Norma Sue slapped him on the back again, so hard this time that if he hadn't been leaning against the breakfast bar, he'd have been knocked back a step or two. "There you go!" she boomed. "Now you're talking. I told them you were too smart a man to miss this opportunity."

"I'm so excited." Esther Mae clasped her hands together as if in prayer. "This is perfect."

"I'll head over there in a few minutes and go ahead and get it done."

"We'll pray for it to all work out." Adela laid her hand back on his forearm and squeezed reassuringly. "I'm feeling very good about this."

"Me, too," Esther Mae gushed, her cheeks pink with excitement. Norma Sue nodded, her eyes glinting with the thrill of a new match being made.

Luke wasn't so sure. He was beginning to think they might be holding out hope for a situation that just might not have the solution they wanted it to have. After Montana's reaction the other night, he kept thinking she was like a skittish colt with open pastures beckoning. But he wasn't a quitter. Not when the prize was right in front of him.

And that meant he had a job to offer the woman he wanted to spend the rest of his life with.

He wanted Montana. For now and for always.

Chapter Twenty

"A job?"

Montana was still shook up about Luke telling her he loved her, and now he was offering her a job? "No, I don't think that would be a very good idea." She'd been checking out the trailer she was going to use to haul Murdock to a rodeo in Stephenville, Texas, that weekend. She'd been startled when Luke had stopped by and dropped this new bombshell of a job on her.

"I know you need help paying for your expenses. And I got to thinking that I need some help with the business. It's growing, and I need professional help with my record keeping and paperwork. Montana, I'm offering you my heart, but since you're not ready for that—" he grinned sheepishly "—then I'm offering you a job instead. Yes, that'll mean you'll be near me and I get to make you fall madly in love with me somewhere along the way. But in the meantime you'll get to support your dream."

Montana tried hard to concentrate on the job part of his pronouncement, and keep her heart out of it. It wasn't helping that he looked nervous. Luke Holden wasn't the nervous type, yet he was right now. And sweet... and dear.

"It would be a win-win for us both," he continued when she didn't say anything.

How could she? Goodness, she loved looking into his eyes. Oh, how she could look at him forever...

No! Stop—she had rodeos to win and roads to travel and dreams to live....

"Tell me more," she forced out. "Though I'm not sure it's good to even think about. I'm afraid you might get hurt in the end—"

He crinkled his forehead. "You let me worry about myself. I'm trying to take care of you."

Montana had a problem. She wanted to throw her arms around him and live happily ever after. She wanted to let him take care of her as he'd said. But that was part of her problem...she needed to do this on her own.

"Luke, I don't want someone to take care of everything," she said more aggressively than she'd meant to. She could tell her tone caught him off guard, but he recovered quickly.

"I didn't mean it literally," Luke said. "I'm not your father. I'm not planning on taking over your life."

"I hate this," Montana groaned, walking down the side of the horse trailer as she tried to fight the sudden flood of anger that surged forward. "I have too much to accomplish, and too much stuff going on inside my head. It hasn't been easy to let things go. I can't set this anger at my father aside. It's there, underlining everything I do."

Luke came up beside her. He looked straight ahead, staring out across the pasture where a group of cattle grazed between two rambling oaks.

"Montana, I hear the bitterness in you. You need to talk about this with your dad and try to resolve it."

"I *can't*. Why is that? Why can't I let go? Why can't I feel joy, reaching for my dreams?" *Or falling in love,* she wanted to add but didn't. She thought, from the shadow of sadness she saw darken Luke's eyes, that he hadn't missed the omission. "Why can't I move on?"

He nudged her shoulder with his own. "I think you're too full of resentment to feel real joy. You have to let it go. That's what I had to do."

She closed her eyes, trying for peace. None came.

"Forgiveness is a tough thing when you don't want to let it go. But it's something you have to do for yourself. And it's something that you have to work at sometimes."

Forgiveness. There it was, she thought with resolve. She'd been pushing it farther and farther back into the shadows, trying to get past it.

She was so angry at her dad that she really didn't want to let the anger go and forgive him. And yet, there was a part of her that did. A part of her that was still his little girl who wanted his love and affection. His approval.

She raised fingers to her temple. Her head was pounding and she felt hot. "I can't do it, Luke."

He turned and dipped his chin, giving her a very frank appraisal. "You can do anything you set your mind to. You're Montana Brown and you're fearless. I've seen you ride." He gave her a devastating smile, his expression so sure.

She couldn't help smiling back, though it was small. "I don't feel fearless. I feel like I can't trust anyone anymore," she whispered.

"You can trust me, Montana. I know your dad let you down. But you can't let his behavior, his choices, affect your life anymore. You have to choose your own path."

"Like you've done?"

He nodded. "I'll admit that I've let my dad's prediction that I'd never amount to anything, that I'd be worthless, drive me all of my life. But I've tried to balance that with God's direction."

"You couldn't be worthless if you tried your hardest. You are worth something wonderful. God didn't make worthless people… they make themselves."

His eyes widened. "See, you do know a thing or two. Exactly. People pick and choose their character and the things that define them. My dad's lack of parenting and love affect my character only as far as I will allow it. When my brothers and I found ourselves basically on our own, I realized I had to make a difference for myself and for them.

I think that's what made my dad despise me so much."

His words cut through her. How could a dad want his son to be worthless? How hard it must have been for Luke. "You are a true survivor, Luke. I respect you so much. But…" she took a deep breath, knowing suddenly that she had to understand about his mother, "…I need to ask you something."

"Anything."

Taking a few strides, she walked to the front of the trailer. There was a flatbed truck parked there, and she sat down on it. Her knees felt weak suddenly. Looking up at Luke, she knew she needed the answers. Needed to understand about his mother more than anything else.

Luke sat beside her.

"I'm serious, Montana, you can trust me. What do you need to know?" He took her hand in his and squeezed it. A million butterflies went crazy in her stomach. The air went light, even though they were sitting in the wide-open breeze.

You love him…

It's impossible not to love him.

Especially when he's squeezing your hand and looking deep into your eyes like now.

Montana closed her eyes and tried to still the voice inside her head. But when she closed her eyes, all she saw was Luke's smiling face.

Luke took Montana's hand and squeezed gently. He wanted to help her move forward. If she could, then maybe they could see where they stood. Montana had grabbed hold of him from the first day, and he hadn't been able to get her off his mind. He couldn't remember if it'd been Sam or App or Stanley who had said it for certain, but he remembered the warning, that one day he wouldn't be able to walk away.

That day had come.

"Montana, I need you to understand that my dad chose his path. He's the one who picked up a bottle. That sounds harsh, but it's true. I have a lot of resentment in me over that. My mom chose to leave, and for the longest time, I had resentment for that, too. But I had little brothers counting on me. And even though I was young, I could still work some and make sure they had food. We didn't always have electricity when I was younger, but we had bread and peanut butter."

Montana's fingers tightened around his and

her eyes glistened. She turned her hand so that she was clutching his. "I hate the picture that paints. I hate that you lived through that."

Looking at her, he was more certain than anything that he loved her. The knowledge sent a thrill of anticipation racing through him. And an even stronger drive to help her past the pain that held her locked in its grip. "I won't kid you, Montana, I hated my dad for the longest time, and I wanted to hate my mother. But Clint's dad, Mac Matlock, helped me realize that we don't get to choose our parents. And sometimes a person doesn't get to choose the decisions that a spouse makes. Spouses can choose to leave for whatever reasons and there isn't anything the other person or the kids can do about it." He paused, remembering how painful it had been learning that lesson. He didn't wish it on anyone.

He gave her an encouraging smile. "Mac taught me what a person can control. What a man is supposed to be. He taught me that a man's character is the only real thing he can control. He did it through demonstration, in being there for his son and making his ranch a success by being honest and having his word mean something. And he did it with a

Bible in his hand. He told me I could choose who I wanted to be, and not let circumstance dictate it for me."

Montana smiled. "You chose to forgive."

"Not as quickly as it seems to you now. Believe me, the Bible is filled with verses about forgiveness, but back then I was like you. I was so angry that I couldn't let myself give it up. Even though I knew that's what God would have me do, I couldn't just do it. But then I understood that I could be like my dad or I could be like Mac. That's when I chose. That's when it turned easy."

"That's why you were so patient with Erica, despite all the rude things she did to you. And that's why you forgave your mother, though she abandoned you."

"Because I chose to. I want to be the kind of man God wants me to be. I don't always make it, but I strive for that. I still have lingering bouts of anger toward my dad. He never regretted what he did to us. That's the difference between him and my mom. She regrets it every day of her life and still does. That's why she won't move here and live on the ranch. She's embarrassed and can't forgive herself."

Luke stood and wrapped Montana up in his arms. She felt so good there with her heart pounding against his. "Let it go, Montana. Make your life your own. Give it to God and then let Him guide you." *And let me love you.*

"Luke, I have a lot to figure out, and my life is about to get more complicated when I hit the rodeo circuit. I'll be gone most of the summer if I'm winning. If I'm going to make the championships, I have to be in the top twenty moneymakers. That means I have to ride everything I can, and as many big money purses as I can make it to. And even then I might not make it."

He placed his hands on his hips, looking unfazed by her ramblings. "Montana, you just ride. You and me, we'll take it one day at a time."

His words were like music to her ears. Montana had to get out of there. "I need to head in." She started walking away as fast as she could. She thought about running, but something had her swinging back around. "Thanks for everything," she said, breathless. There was so much to get done and so little time. She had to hit the road. She had to leave all of this behind and she had to win.

"Hey," he called. "I planned to tell you I'm going to meet Colt between here and the Oklahoma border tomorrow. I had planned to support you and watch you ride, but he needs me to bring him some of his gear. He's not going to have time to swing by and pick it up before heading to Reno."

Again the cowboy knew how to get to her. "You don't need to come see me. I'm fine, and Colt needs you. How's he doing?"

"He's worn slap out, but he's been winning, and that's what he wants. You know how that is."

She smiled. "Yup. At least I hope to. Hauling from rodeo to rodeo was hard, but state-to-state running for the big money was killer. A friend and I did it during the summer of my senior year before getting out of high school. I loved it, but still remember the endless road passing under our wheels. Thankfully, I didn't have to do the driving back then. This is going be different."

"I hate the idea of you on the road by yourself—" Luke stopped himself. He didn't like it one bit, but that wasn't his call and he knew it. "Sorry." He longed to hug her and assure her that all would be fine. But she didn't need to be crowded any more than he'd already done. "Get some rest. You're going to need it," was all he would let himself say.

"Thanks," she answered, turned and walked away.

He wanted to believe everything was going to turn out fine. Talk about trusting God…he had to do it. But as he watched her go, something just didn't feel right.

If she was winning, then that meant she was going to be on the road, not here in Mule Hollow. Not here, where he could woo her.

Chapter Twenty-One

Montana maneuvered her trailer into a parking spot at the back of the lot. She was here. It had been a pretty good drive from Mule Hollow to Stephenville. Hopping from the cab, she jogged to the back of the trailer, anxious to get Murdock unloaded so she could head up to the announcer's box to check out the order of events and see where they had her in the lineup. She knew the barrels would be toward the end of the rodeo, most likely right before the bull competition.

"Hey, big fella," she said, as she led Murdock from the trailer. He pawed the ground as soon as he was outside. This felt great. A group of young cowgirls walking by were laughing and having a great time. Their excited voices rang out as they went. It reminded her of when she'd competed during high school. Back in the days when she was determined to be the best barrel racer there had ever been.

The thought made her smile as she headed toward the announcer's box. She had been so young back then.

She wondered what Luke was doing. Her mind had drifted to him at random moments throughout her drive. He was never far from her thoughts. Several times she even pulled her cell phone out to call him. But she didn't.

In Mule Hollow, she wouldn't be able to reach him with her cell phone, but now she knew they were only a call away from each other.

She wondered if he'd thought about calling her.

Happy with the next-to-last spot on the list, she left the building, heading back toward Murdock and nearly jumped out of her boots when her phone rang. It hadn't rung the entire time that she'd been in Mule Hollow. The service was so bad in the tiny town that she'd even stopped carrying it. She'd only attached it to her belt because she'd been traveling.

"Hello," she said without glancing at the caller ID.

"Montana, this is your father."

She froze. She didn't know what to do. A slow internal vibration seemed to start deep inside of her as the anger and betrayal she'd been suppressing coiled more tightly.

"Hi." Amazingly, her voice didn't shake. There was no emotion at all. Her fingers tightened in conjunction with her insides, despite the emotional onslaught. It was hard calling him Daddy when she was so sick at heart. Her stomach rolled at the sound of his voice, though a part of her longed for all of what had transpired to go away. Longed for things to be back to normal.

Her mother was moving forward. Strange that she'd seemed better able to handle her father's betrayal than Montana was.

"Montana, when are you coming back home and taking your responsibility to this company seriously? I understand you took a few weeks off to come to terms with what's happened. But it's time for you to get back to work. People are depending on you."

There was no remorse or apology. There was only family responsibility—*her* family responsibility. None of his. She gritted her teeth and held back the high boil of her temper, counting to three—no way could she have made it to ten!

"Dad, I'm not coming back." It felt good, as the words came out sure and true.

"Montana…"

"Dad, I chose accounting for you and I can't do it any longer."

"Montana, you are taking what has happened between your mother and me far too personally. You are using it as an excuse to relinquish your responsibilities."

"No, Dad, I'm not. It's just time for me to do what *I* want."

Silence filled the space between them. In her mind's eye, she could see her father's lips flatten out in displeasure. She'd never liked seeing that look on his face. She'd always tried to make him smile, even at the expense of not doing what she wanted. It hit her, looking back, how selfish her father was.

"It's time for you to grow up, Montana. I've built this firm for you to take over someday. It's time for you to come back here and act responsible in front of the employees. I've been patient. Your mother and I are moving on. It's time for you to understand that. It's time for you to put this cowgirl nonsense out of your mind and come back here and tend to your responsibilities. And I mean now." Then the line went dead. Her father had made his demands and then hung up on her.

Montana just stood there in disbelief, holding the phone to her ear. Closing her eyes, she tried to calm down. She wished Luke was near so she could talk to him. Wished she could feel his reassuring embrace.

After all that her dad had done...after all the pain he'd inflicted on his family, he had called her dream nonsense? Told her she was being selfish?

Her dreams weren't nonsense. They weren't worthless.

"You okay?" a cowboy asked as he was passing by. "You look like you're going to pass out."

Montana gave him a tight smile. "I'm fine. Thanks."

He grinned. "Nerves will do that to you sometimes. Take a few breaths before you get out there, and you'll be fine."

Montana smiled and watched the pleasant cowboy head inside. Missing Luke all the more, she turned and headed back to get Murdock ready.

You have to forgive your dad, Montana. For your own good. Luke's words came back to her as she went. Her dad, so selfish and self-centered…and she was supposed to forgive him?

Let go of the bitterness. Choose who you want to be.

Montana stopped cold in her tracks. She was standing on the sidewalk before the parking lot, and it hit her—she didn't want to be angry anymore.

She didn't want her life to be dictated by her father or the anger she felt toward him.

She wanted to be the woman God had intended her to be. She wanted to let it go and be free of the heavy weight she'd been carrying around on her shoulders. It was unbelievable!

She needed to talk to Luke. She dialed his number, noticing a cowboy moving toward her from the direction where her truck was parked. He moved with a familiar gait. His hat shadowed his face, his dark hair curled from beneath it, and she knew… "Luke!" she called, beginning to walk toward the cowboy. She knew it was him. "Luke!" she exclaimed, knowing him anywhere. Her heart knew him, too, and lunged against her chest.

Realizing he might not see her for the cars splattered across the parking lot, she started running. Dashing off the sidewalk, she emerged from behind a trailer into the open. She waved as she ran, so excited to see him. "Luke—"

She never saw the truck blasting from around the corner of the building...until she heard the squeal of its brakes...

"Montana, can you hear me?" Luke couldn't think straight as he knelt beside her. She'd been looking at him when the truck came plowing around the corner. It stopped before it ran over her, but there had been contact. Montana was thumped hard by the truck, and sent flying to the pavement.

"Man, I'm sorry! I didn't see her."

Luke looked up at the young cowboy who'd jumped from the truck and was about to pass out with worry.

Montana started to sit up, but Luke held her down. "Stay down," he commanded, as she looked straight at him.

"What are you doing here?" she asked.

"I came to see you ride, and you almost killed yourself in front of me?"

"Do I need to call the paramedics?" the cowboy asked, hopping from one boot to the other. "She's bleeding. See her arm—oh, man, oh, man it's bleeding. And she hit her head on the truck before she fell."

"No, I can get u—"

"Please call them," Luke cut her off, looking at her scraped hands and the tear in her jeans. This was worse than the time she fell off of Murdock. And she'd hit her head on the hood when she buckled forward. Luke was glad her eyes seemed clear. He didn't think the hit had been that hard, but they weren't taking any chances. "You stay put," he said when Montana tried to sit up again.

"I'm fine. I'll be ready to ride here in just a little while. I need to sit up and talk to you. I'm so glad you're here."

That sent a thrill racing through him. "You were hit by a truck, Montana, so don't move."

She gave him a dazzling smile as she looked up at him. "Okay, whatever you say."

Her easy agreement had him worrying about a concussion. He didn't see any lump forming on her forehead, so maybe she'd hit it harder than he thought.

"Does your head hurt?" he asked, leaning closer, to see if there was an injury of some kind that he was missing.

"Nope. I love you, Luke."

Her words froze him. He knelt beside her

and he couldn't move. "You said you loved me? Just how many of me do you see?" he asked, figuring she'd had something knocked loose.

A slow smile spread over her face. "I see one of you, but I think you're worth twenty."

The crowd that had formed around them oohed over that statement, and he had to chuckle. "Okay, where's Montana Brown?" he asked, as the rodeo paramedics drove up in their ambulance and hopped out.

For the next twenty minutes Montana entertained the crowd and the paramedics. He was surprised when they bandaged up a few cuts and let her go.

"You'll probably be pretty sore tomorrow," one of them said, "but it's a wonder nothing was broken." They drove them over to her trailer and Luke helped her out. Then she waved to the paramedics as they drove off.

"Whew, I'm glad that's over," she said, winking at him.

Unable to hold back any longer, he pulled her carefully into his arms. "Montana, you scared me senseless."

She laid her head on his chest. "Sorry. I got a little reckless when I saw you. But you were supposed to be with Colt." She hugged him hard.

He pushed a loose strand of hair behind her ear and kissed her forehead. Thankful she was okay.

"I'm so glad you came. But what about Colt?"

Her words meant more to him than she could know. "He ended up being delayed a day, so I was only a couple of hours away from you—easy choice, I came to see you. I got here early and thought I'd surprise you. Little did I know you were going to throw yourself in front of a moving truck."

She chuckled despite the seriousness of the accident. He was sure the laugh was a release of tension more than anything.

A patient Murdock watched them with an expectant expression. The horse was ready to compete, just like Montana was. They were going to do well; he felt it.

"Luke," she said, not moving her head from his chest. "I told you I loved you earlier."

He stilled, trying to be nonchalant about it. "Yeah, I know. That's why I knew you'd had a hard lick."

She leaned back and held his gaze. "Not

such a hard lick. I knew exactly what I was saying. That's what I was coming to tell you when I got hit."

"I think I need to sit down."

She gave a light chuckle as he reached for the door handle and pulled the back door open. Immediately, he sank to the seat, hanging on to her as he did. If he had his way, he wasn't ever letting her go. Not after what she'd just said.

"I love you, Montana, with all my heart. But what's happened? Why this sudden change of attitude?"

"My dad called and demanded that I come back to the firm because of my family obligations. He called my dreams nonsense and he took no responsibility for his actions. I was so angry, and then it hit me. I could hear you and God both telling me to let it go. I realized I didn't want all that anger hanging on me like weights. I wanted to feel free and happy. I wanted to know that I was in control of my life where my attitude and character are concerned. And above all, I knew God was in control. So I let it go, I let it all go. And I felt great. Then I wanted to see you so bad. I needed to share it with you, and then there you were! It was like a dream. I just couldn't believe you showed up. I still can't believe it."

He grinned at the joy in her words. "I'm so glad you're letting this anger go. One day, maybe you'll be able to mend fences with your dad. Letting the anger go and forgiving him is a way to open the door for that to happen. I'm proud of you. I knew you could do it."

She smiled. "I like that. I could get used to making you proud of me."

He laughed, feeling great. Then he sobered. "Do you think you could ever get used to living the rest of your life with me—you know, with the whole package, marriage, babies and a few National Rodeo Championships?"

She snuggled in close, hugging him tightly. "I would love it. But we'd have to have a plan."

"It can be done," he said, unable to believe he was hearing her right.

They grinned at each other, basking in the moment. He gently tugged on her braid. "I don't think that would be a problem at all," he said, and then he did what he'd been waiting to do—he lowered his lips to hers.

Montana kissed him, then sighed against his lips. "Life is good, isn't it, Luke?"

"It gets better by the moment. I love you, Montana Brown."

"And that is exactly what I've been needing to hear."

"I hope so, because you're going to be hearing it a lot."

"Bring it on, cowboy." She laughed. Murdock pawed the earth and snorted. "Okay, it's time to roll." She looked from Murdock to Luke. "You with me?"

Luke's heart was pounding with love and expectation of the future that lay ahead. "I'm with you, now and forever, cowgirl of mine."

Montana grinned. "Now *that's* what I like to hear!"

* * * * *

Dear Reader,

I hope you enjoyed *Her Rodeo Cowboy*. I'm always thrilled when readers choose to spend time in Mule Hollow with me and the Mule Hollow gang.

I loved the man that Luke was in this book. He didn't let the bad in his life determine who he became, but instead, he became the man *he* wanted to become—the kind of man that he'd needed in his life as a child and hadn't been blessed to have. He became someone others could depend on. Montana needed that kind of man in her life now, and she needed the folks of Mule Hollow, too. Isn't it wonderful how God puts just what we need into our paths, just when we need it? I pray that you'll be just what someone needs in a time of need…or that if you are in need, that God will place just the right person in your path to help you. He has done it for me so many times.

I hope you'll join me in the next few months for the two Mule Hollow Homecoming books. They will be Jess Holden and Colt Holden's stories. I don't always get to write back, but I try. Still, I love hearing from readers. You can reach me at P.O. Box 1125 Madisonville TX 77864 or debraclopton.com.

Until the next time, live, laugh and seek God with all your heart,

Debra Clopton

Questions for Discussions

1. Luke wasn't thinking about getting married at all. He was just interested in making his ranch into a success. Why was that?

2. Do you think that Montana was overreacting to her parents' divorce? Why do you think Montana was having such a hard time with her parents' divorce, especially at her age?

3. Why did Lacy want Montana to come stay with her and her family? Was it just to be a babysitter for Tate? Or did she have something else in mind for Montana?

4. Why do you think the matchmakers are so obsessed with fixing up the single people in town?

5. When Stanley was ill, Montana made it a point to go over to his house and take him some soup. What does that say about her?

6. Did you think Montana was being a bit hard on Luke when she told him she didn't want to be just one of the many women he's dated? Have you ever judged someone too harshly?

7. What did you think about Erica? Do you think Luke was in the right about how he handled the situation?

8. Have you ever had to figure out a way to deal with someone difficult, someone who refused to cooperate in any way? How did that turn out?

9. Montana gave up her dream to be a barrel racer because her father wanted her to. Would you have done the same thing or done things differently? Why?

10. Luke didn't let his past be an excuse to fail. Instead, he aimed to achieve all he could and become a man others could look up to. What do you think of this? Do you know any people who are like him? Please describe.

11. Montana had a problem letting herself trust a man after losing faith in her father.

But God, in His faithfulness, put a man in her path who was more than she believed a man could be. Do you believe there are men out there like Luke? Do you know any? Discuss.

LARGER-PRINT BOOKS!

**GET 2 FREE
LARGER-PRINT NOVELS
PLUS 2 FREE
MYSTERY GIFTS**

Love Inspired

Larger-print novels are now available...

YES! Please send me 2 FREE LARGER-PRINT Love Inspired® novels and my 2 FREE mystery gifts (gifts are worth about $10). After receiving them, if I don't wish to receive any more books, I can return the shipping statement marked "cancel". If I don't cancel, I will receive 6 brand-new novels every month and be billed just $4.99 per book in the U.S. or $5.49 per book in Canada. That's a saving of at least 23% off the cover price. It's quite a bargain! Shipping and handling is just 50¢ per book in the U.S. and 75¢ per book in Canada.* I understand that accepting the 2 free books and gifts places me under no obligation to buy anything. I can always return a shipment and cancel at any time. Even if I never buy another book, the two free books and gifts are mine to keep forever.

122/322 IDN FEG3

Name	(PLEASE PRINT)	

Address		Apt. #

City	State/Prov.	Zip/Postal Code

Signature (if under 18, a parent or guardian must sign)

Mail to the **Reader Service:**
IN U.S.A.: P.O. Box 1867, Buffalo, NY 14240-1867
IN CANADA: P.O. Box 609, Fort Erie, Ontario L2A 5X3

Not valid to current subscribers to Love Inspired Larger-Print books.

**Are you a current subscriber to Love Inspired books
and want to receive the larger-print edition?
Call 1-800-873-8635 or visit www.ReaderService.com.**

* Terms and prices subject to change without notice. Prices do not include applicable taxes. Sales tax applicable in N.Y. Canadian residents will be charged applicable taxes. Offer not valid in Quebec. This offer is limited to one order per household. All orders subject to credit approval. Credit or debit balances in a customer's account(s) may be offset by any other outstanding balance owed by or to the customer. Please allow 4 to 6 weeks for delivery. Offer available while quantities last.

Your Privacy—The Reader Service is committed to protecting your privacy. Our Privacy Policy is available online at www.ReaderService.com or upon request from the Reader Service.

We make a portion of our mailing list available to reputable third parties that offer products we believe may interest you. If you prefer that we not exchange your name with third parties, or if you wish to clarify or modify your communication preferences, please visit us at www.ReaderService.com/consumerschoice or write to us at Reader Service Preference Service, P.O. Box 9062, Buffalo, NY 14269. Include your complete name and address.

LILP11B

Love Inspired®
SUSPENSE
RIVETING INSPIRATIONAL ROMANCE

Watch for our series of edge-
of-your-seat suspense novels.
These contemporary tales
of intrigue and romance
feature Christian characters
facing challenges to their faith...
and their lives!

AVAILABLE IN REGULAR
& LARGER-PRINT FORMATS

For exciting stories that reflect traditional values,
visit:
www.ReaderService.com